# FAT VAMPIRE
by Johnny B. Truant

## Johnny B. Truant's
# FAT VAMPIRE

# A NOTE ABOUT THIS BOOK

I'm one of the three hosts of a podcast called *Better Off Undead* (which you can find at betteroffundeadshow.com and all the usual podcast places) and on episode 6 of that podcast, we asked the question, "If a vampire offered to turn you into one of his kind, would you accept?"

Dave, our resident "fat guy and proud of it," said that he'd take the deal.

My co-host Sean and I said that maybe that wouldn't be such a great idea for Dave, because if you're out of shape when you're turned, you might stay out of shape for all of eternity.

So I wrote a whole series of books about that single dumb idea, and what you're about to read is the first of them.

**Enjoy.**

For all the fat vampires out there.

# FAT VAMPIRE
by Johnny B. Truant

# ASSHOLE

REGINALD BASKIN, NOT REMOTELY A religious man, closed his eyes in his small cubicle and asked God for his money back.

"Whatever I paid before I was a sperm, Lord," he said under his breath, "I want it back. Every cent, or I'm reporting your ass to the Better Business Bureau. I was promised much that I did not receive. The marketing was deceptive. I am not completely satisfied. I would like a full refund and a personal apology from the maitre d'. And a free calendar. Not a shitty one. One with naked girls on it."

Reginald was many things. He'd been the fat kid in high school. He'd been the fat kid who didn't fit into the small lecture hall seats and had to sit in the aisle in college. He was now the fat guy who worked for a fitness equipment manufacturer, which had its own unique breed of irony. He was also, on occasion, the fat guy on the bus and the fat guy who wouldn't take his shirt off at the beach.

And he was, lastly, the kind of person who prayed out loud to a god he didn't believe in when nobody could hear him but himself, just to prove a point.

Reginald stood up, leaning heavily on the corner of his desk to do so. He looked down at his wheeled chair, grabbed the small pink set of rubber lips that was protruding from under his seat cushion, and pulled.

A Whoopee Cushion. Awesome.

He dropped the thing into the trash can, then sat back down and tried to ignore the snickers coming from the other side of the cubicle wall.

Fucking Todd Walker.

He wouldn't give him the satisfaction of replying, of rebutting, or of responding. He'd just act as if nothing had happened. There had *been* no farting noise and no unceremonious disposal into the trash can. *Screw you, Walker. I didn't even notice your prank.*

Walker had never grown up; that was the problem. Neither had Simmons or Yancy or McGuinness or Graham or Nichols or any of the rest of the sales team. Almost the entire company was male, in its 20s, and in great shape as befitted a proper fitness company. The only exceptions were those who worked behind the scenes: Reginald, Sarah Kopke, Noel Leonard, Scott Valentine, and the new kid who worked overnight and dressed all in black. Everyone else looked alike and was more or less ready for a magazine cover shoot on a moment's notice, should the need arise.

Reginald was fat. Sarah and Noel weren't terribly attractive and were the wrong gender. Scott was in his sixties. The new kid looked nineteen if he were a day, and dressed like a goth. He wore a sword on his belt, for God's sake. Nobody wanted to talk to him.

But everyone else looked alike, as if they'd been cast from the same mold. Reginald, Sarah, Noel, Scott, and the new kid couldn't've stood out more if they'd tried, and just like in high school, standing out meant Whoopee Cushions on your chair or dentures and adult diapers on your desk. Or, if you were especially lucky, tampons in your coffee.

It was enough to make you ask for your money back.

Reginald had always held onto hope. He'd taken the abuse all through high school with as much aplomb as he could because it was always only a few more years, months, and days until he was out of school, into college, and into the real world where people understood that appearances only ran skin deep. But that's not what had happened. Instead of landing in a nonjudgmental utopia, he'd landed in a frat house.

He wondered if it would always be like this. He wondered if people ever changed. He wondered if he could ever be just "Reginald" instead of "Reginald the fat guy."

Across the cubicle wall came a farting noise. Then another. Then another and another and another in rapid succession, counterpointed with the guffaws and chortling of two deep male voices.

Apparently the Whoopee Cushions had been a two-for-one deal.

This wasn't supposed to be the deal. This wasn't what he'd signed up for.

# IT GUY

THE NEW KID, WHO WORKED in IT and kept the computers working, turned out to be named Maurice. Reginald felt bad for him. The kid was asking for it by being nineteen. He was asking for it by being a small, shy goth boy with black hair and black clothes and black nail polish. But he was really asking for it — like, *above and beyond* asking for it — by being named *Maurice*.

For some reason, the perpetually teenaged found name humor especially poignant. One of Reginald's best friends in high school had the misfortune of being named "Tag," and being in the chess club. From ninth through twelfth grades, Tag was "Fag." Sometimes teachers even said it wrong because the football players were good at internal branding.

Not that Maurice rhymed with anything interesting — or at least not anything in the vocabulary range of the clones — but it was very French. It was the sort of name you'd knock a kid's books out from under his arm for having.

Still, despite their shared foes, Reginald didn't want to talk to Maurice. Maurice was weird even from Reginald's perspective. He was a goth, for one. He wore that sword on his belt, which *had* to be against human resources' policy. He never seemed to eat or drink. He had brought in a special chair that he kind of kneeled on and that had no back on it. His hair was always over his face.

But one day, Reginald found himself in the kitchen with the kid and felt he had to say something, because it was awkward not to.

"Hey," said Reginald.

"Hey," said Maurice.

Things became less awkward after that. The next time Reginald ran into Maurice, he said "Hey" again and Maurice said "What's up?" Reginald decided the question was rhetorical and that he probably wasn't expected to explain what was actually up, but it was nice to have someone feigning interest for a change. It was so much better than being shoved into walls as he walked and told that he was taking up too much hallway.

The next time he saw Maurice, it was Maurice who initiated the conversation.

"What's up?" said Maurice

"What's up," countered Reginald, leaving the question mark off the end to affect the disinterest that Maurice seemed so interested in.

It was nice to have a friend in the office.

Sarah and Noel, the company's only two women, didn't understand the new kid. They had both had their perception of attractiveness shattered by the company's homogenous appearance. The problem was that while the rest of the men in the company were indeed universally attractive, their attractiveness went hand-in-hand with a breed of overt chauvinism that hadn't been popular since the 1950s. Reginald had a few armchair-psychology theories about Sarah and Noel. He figured they were searching for someone to be attracted to who wasn't attractive enough to be a total asshole. But Maurice might be too far in the other direction. Maurice confused them.

"I think he's gay," Reginald heard Sarah say while he was heating up a French bread pizza in the toaster oven.

"Oh, of course he is," said Noel. "I mean, his name is *Maurice*."

"I don't think he's gay," said Reginald.

Noel looked at Reginald as if she'd been slapped. Culture at the company wasn't exactly full of camaraderie outside of the six-pack-abs set, so entering a conversation that you'd overheard but hadn't been invited to join was sort of like peeing in someone's coffee while they stood there and watched you do it.

Noel seemed to think that she should respond, so she said, "Why don't you think he's gay?"

"I don't know. I just don't get that vibe."

"What would you know?" said Sarah. "You're a man, and you're not gay."

"How do you know I'm not gay?" said Reginald, who wasn't gay but who didn't care if anyone thought he was.

The thing about Sarah, Noel, Scott, and Maurice was that although they were mostly apathetic about each other and about Reginald, all five were united by their shared loathing of Walker and his clones. Noel, Scott, Sarah, and (probably) Maurice would never say that Reginald was fat, mock his fat, or even comment, when asked about him by a third party, that he was fat. And Reginald, for his part, felt the same about them. Scott wasn't *old*, for instance. He was *Scott*, and he wasn't part of the army of clones. That was enough.

"Women can sense these things," said Sarah.

"Would you ask him out, if you didn't think he was gay?" said Reginald. It was an odd question, totally out of character for him to ask. Really, it was out of character for Reginald to ask anything. Really, it was out of character for anyone other than the clones to ask anyone anything at all. Except "for permission."

"I don't know," said Sarah. "He seems moody."

"He's awfully young," said Noel.

"So you'd date him if you were nineteen?" said Reginald.

"I'm glad I'm not nineteen anymore," said Sarah with a shiver. She had a lazy eye. Like Reginald, she'd simply endured high school, waiting for it to end so that she could move into the adult world where people were civilized. Reginald could tell by the way she jumped when anyone dropped anything that she wanted her money back for the broken promises of adulthood too.

"I guess," said Sarah.

Despite the lazy eye, Sarah was attractive. She didn't know it, though, and she hid it well. She had no sense of cosmetics and seemed to know just enough about haircare to get her by. Her dark brown hair was always in a tidy but uninteresting bun, and her wardrobe was comprised of dumpy slacks and out-of-style blouses. She turned to Reginald. "Would *you*, if *you* were gay and nineteen?"

This line of discussion was strange, but Reginald liked it. He never talked to the others in the office. Sometimes he wondered why, given that they were all outcasts. He supposed it was due to the office's atmosphere of oppression. The proles in *1984* probably didn't engage in much small talk either.

"If I was gay and nineteen, sure," said Reginald.

"Someone has a man crush," said Sarah.

Reginald shrugged. He almost said what was on his lips, which was *I don't have many friends.* But in addition to being untrue (he had his family and the four guys he played poker with sometimes), it sounded pathetic. He was already cubbyholed as pathetic for being so fat, and he didn't need another crucifixion stake floating around, waiting to be picked up.

The kitchen door opened and a cleft chin with a set of perfect teeth walked in. It took Reginald a moment to decide exactly who it was because the rest of the office looked so much alike, but eventually he saw that it was Todd Walker. Once he did, he became very interested in the coffee he was stirring.

"You in here again, Reggie?" said Walker, who knew that Reginald hated being called "Reggie." "Damn, boy, give the fridge some time off!"

"I was only grabbing…"

"Just busting your balls," said Walker, slapping him on the back. Then, in an aside tone of voice: "Assuming I can find them in there." He chortled again to show that it was just a joke, which of course it wasn't.

"That's not nice," said Sarah.

"Oh, he knows I'm only kidding. And who knows? Maybe one day we'll make a success story out of Reggie like that Jared guy from Subway, and then we'll all get rich selling the shit out of these treadmills." Walker smiled. His teeth looked like Arlington tombstones.

Walker grabbed a protein bar out of the refrigerator.

"What you all pow-wowing about in here?" he said.

Nobody answered. Sarah was dissecting her French bread pizza like it was a pithed frog in science class.

"C'mon. Noel, what were you guys talking about?"

Noel looked up. "The new guy."

Walker made an odd frown that only happened on half of his mouth, like the other half didn't get the memo. "That fucker's weird." He took a bite of the protein bar, then continued with a mouthful of soy or whey or whatever it was. "That sword. I'm worried he's going to snap. I asked him about it and he said he uses it to trim his hedges. Think he's serious?" He didn't pause to let anyone answer. "Saw him leaving a few times when I came in to the office in the morning. So he works all night, and when he leaves, you know what he does? He walks home, and he wears a coat with a hood, and he — get this —" Walker laughed, because clearly everyone would want to mock the following point. "— he carries an umbrella. Like a parasol."

Walker, his mouth full of protein bar and his perfect white teeth fighting to be seen amidst the food, looked at Reginald so that he could confirm how crazy the IT guy was.

Reginald shrugged.

Walker closed his mouth and shrugged back. "Maybe you don't think it's strange, but you're not exactly in the middle of the bell curve." He took another bite.

Noel coughed, then covered her mouth quickly and resumed looking at her lunch.

"Well, I've gotta get to work. Trying to leave early. Have a date with a contortionist who can put her legs behind her head and cross them like a pretzel." He leered at Sarah and Noel, both of whom might be prospects for Walker if they underwent an extreme makeover. "Can either of you do that?" he said with an erect penis in his voice.

And with that, Walker was gone. The earlier spirit of loose camaraderie left with him.

Then Sarah spoke. "I wonder if he has a skin condition or something," she said. "Maurice, I mean."

Reginald turned to go. "Maybe he's a vampire," he said with a chuckle, and then he let the kitchen door close behind him and walked back to his desk.

# BRO DATE

MAURICE WORKED FROM 11PM UNTIL 8am with, presumably, an hour break for what Reginald had to assume he called "lunch." His job seemed to be doing a lot of technical stuff that Reginald didn't understand and didn't particularly care about.

After a few weeks, Reginald's rut began to settle into a familiar rhythm of intersection with Maurice's rut. They started to run into each other at precisely 7am each morning when Reginald, who preferred to get in early and get out early, walked down to the kitchen for his second cup of coffee. That's where he found Maurice one day, sitting at one of the tables with a cellular phone in his hands, using both of his thumbs to text or email someone at an inhuman speed.

"Holy crap are you fast on that keyboard," said Reginald. Then, deciding to go for broke with his new office "friend," he added, "My fingers are too big for one of those things, but even on a regular-sized keyboard I'm pretty slow."

Maurice jerked his head around and uttered a noise of surprise. The door had been propped open and he hadn't seen Reginald enter.

13

"I'm sorry," said Reginald. "Thought you saw me here."

"Nah, it's... it's cool," said Maurice, stowing the phone with a self-conscious glance around as if he'd been caught doing something private, lewd, or both. He paused, then answered Reginald's observation: "Practice texting is all."

"You work at night, right?" said Reginald. He didn't wait for an answer because he was only making preamble. "So when you take your hour break, do you call it 'lunch' even though it's like 3am?"

Maurice nodded. "Yeah," he said.

"So do you eat lunch foods, or is it, like, your dinner?"

Maurice's mouth made an amused half-smile. "I just grab a quick bite," he said.

"And so, if you work at night, how do you have a social life?" Then he realized how forward that question was, especially with the corporate culture being what it was, and muttered an apology. It was the fact that the clones weren't here, he realized. None of them arrived before 8am, and most arrived closer to 8:30 or 9. These were the sweetest hours of the day — another reason he liked to come in early.

"It's cool," said Maurice. "I don't mind you asking. And to answer your question, the truth is that I *don't* have much of a social life. It's one of the downsides of living how I do."

"Maybe we could hang out," Reginald blurted. It was out before he gave himself permission to say it, and he immediately regretted it. Maybe he did have a man crush. This was odd of him, odd at the office, and odd in a dozen other ways.

"Sure," said Maurice. "It'd have to be right before I get to work, though. Like nine or ten at night. I get up around eight PM, and, honestly, I can't get much sun." He shrugged. "I've got a condition."

"That'd be cool," said Reginald. *Cool.* The word felt foreign on his lips. It was something he never had been, and definitely was not currently. "Let's do that sometime."

"Cool," said Maurice. He stood to go, tipping an invisible hat at Reginald and then stepping sideways to move his skinny frame around Reginald's formidable protruding stomach. He didn't ask Reginald to move aside, even in a polite way, and made no show of holding his own tiny gut in as he passed. Reginald silently thanked him for the courtesy.

When Maurice was halfway down the hallway, Reginald decided, in the spirit of the moment, to ask one final question.

"Hey," he said. "Why do you wear a sword on your belt?"

"I use it to trim my hedges," said Maurice.

He waved and was gone. For some reason, Reginald decided he was dead serious.

# BABES

REGINALD DIDN'T BUG MAURICE ABOUT setting a time to hang out. He felt odd having proposed a bro date in the first place, and he wasn't used to not being laughed at. He figured he'd let the idea simmer. Either Maurice was genuinely interested in hanging out or he was just being polite. If the latter was true, Maurice would never propose a time and Reginald would give himself the dignity of never raising the issue. But as it was, Maurice turned out to be genuinely interested, and surprised him the next Monday by suggesting they go bowling.

They settled on meeting at the lanes at 9pm — a full two-meal cycle after work for Reginald and two hours before work for Maurice. Reginald was surprised that Maurice had suggested bowling. He half figured they'd end up using a Ouija board or attending a black opera. Something as normal as bowling coming from the sword-wielding goth kid was a welcome surprise.

Reginald hadn't bowled in years, but he'd been good back in high school despite already being over two hundred and fifty pounds. Now, a hundred pounds heavier and with foot trouble, back trouble, high cholesterol, and (he was pretty sure) pre-diabetes, bowling was still within his physical capabilities. It was physical but not taxing, and the lane balls came in a wide range of weights and finger-hole sizes. As a plus, a bro date involving bowling wasn't awkwardly intimate like dinner or loud like going to a bar — which for Reginald would also be totally uninteresting because he was a teetotaler.

Yes, bowling would do just fine.

They were three frames into the first game when Maurice seemed to hear something, looked toward the entrance, and groaned.

Reginald raised his head and followed Maurice's gaze. At first, he thought that Walker and his clones had gotten into character and followed them to the bowling alley, but then he realized it was an entirely different group of perfect people.

It was Maurice's own collection of Todd Walker clones.

The group was comprised of two couples that appeared to be in their early twenties. All four were supernaturally beautiful. The women's hair (identical in style, though one was blonde and one was a deep chestnut) was perfectly groomed and styled, shiny and bouncy, seeming to move in a breeze that didn't exist. The cheekbones on all four were high and perfectly set. The men had a sixteenth inch of stubble that didn't look shaggy, but instead looked stylish and handsome. They were somehow both rugged and feminine, like they could chop some serious wood, but could do so without ruining their nails or knocking a hair out of their perfect cover-model hairdos.

All four were dressed like Maurice — full black coats with black clothes underneath. They even wore black nail polish, and the women wore black lipstick. The only difference between their black clothes and Maurice's black clothes was the cut. What the four beautiful people were wearing was chic and at the height of couture. What Maurice wore looked practical. Where Maurice looked morose, the four newcomers looked like European runway models.

"Friends of yours?" said Reginald.

"Hardly," said Maurice. He made eye contact with one of the men, who'd spotted him and was leading the group over.

Maurice stood and met them halfway between the lanes and the door. All five of them stood in a scrum, twenty feet from Reginald. Maurice looked small and shabby next to the others. It was as if they were all siblings in a high-class litter of dogs, and Maurice was the runt. Reginald tried not to watch them out of courtesy, but he couldn't help staring at the women. They were astonishingly beautiful. Like dark angels, they were.

After a few minutes of what looked like argumentative discussion, Maurice walked over to Reginald and said, "Sorry about this. I need to handle something. It shouldn't take long."

The blonde woman was looking at Reginald. She was licking her lips. His first thought was that she was mocking him — someone as attractive as she was couldn't possibly be attracted to someone like him — but then he noticed that the other woman was doing the same. Then, putting a new point on the whole experience, he noticed that the men were doing it, too.

The blonde woman raised her hand and made a slow beckoning gesture with one delicate finger. Reginald didn't consider refusing. His legs propped him up as if of their own will and he found himself standing beside her before he knew what had happened.

The woman looked at Maurice. "I want him to come with us," she said. Then, to Reginald: "What's your name, big boy?"

"Reginald."

"Nice to meet you, Reginald," she purred. "I'm Moira." She extended a hand. The gesture was feline. It almost felt as if she expected him to kiss it and he actually felt himself bending at the waist to obey, but then he caught Maurice's eye and simply shook the beautiful hand. She lowered it slowly, her eyes never leaving his.

He was beginning to feel lightheaded, as if he were intoxicated.

"Moira," said Maurice. "Knock it off."

The woman looked away, at Maurice. Reginald felt his environment return like a splash of cold water. It was as if a spell had been broken.

"Is he yours?" she asked Maurice.

The question seemed to embarrass Maurice. "We're just hanging out," he said.

"Then maybe he'd like to be mine," said the woman with the chestnut hair, running a finger along his shoulder.

Reginald felt his chest rise.

"Or mine," said one of the men.

Reginald felt his chest fall.

There was a moment of silence, and then Maurice stepped between the group and Reginald. He did it with the air of an older brother breaking up some kind of idiocy being perpetrated by siblings, but it was strange because the others were all at least four or five years older than he was.

"Reginald, this is Moira, Penelope, Charles, and Isaac. We have a... a kind of working arrangement. They need a few minutes of my time."

"He's been *naughty*," said the one Maurice had called Penelope, running a finger down Reginald's neck.

Moira whispered in his ear. "He's been *baaaaad...*"

Maurice shook his head, exasperated.

"Charles and Isaac need to spend a few minutes with me out back, trying to intimidate me and pretending they can tell me what to do," said Maurice, his eyes on Charles. "But then they'll run on home like good little errand boys and we can finish our game. Isn't that right, kids?"

It was odd to hear so young of a man call the others "kids" and speak to them so disrespectfully. There was some odd subtext beneath what Maurice and the others were saying that Reginald didn't understand. Maurice seemed to be speaking with a double-meaning on purpose, knowing that it would mean nothing to Reginald but unable to stop himself from doing it anyway. Reginald was reminded of himself asking God, out loud, for his money back when Walker had put the Whoopee Cushion on his seat.

But what was most interesting to Reginald was that Maurice, who was smaller and younger than the others, was clearly in charge of whatever was happening. Isaac and Charles *thought* that they were in charge, but they were wrong.

"Okay," said Reginald. "Do what you need to do. I'll stay here."

"The women are staying here," said Maurice.

"Okay," said Reginald with enthusiasm.

"So you'd better come with us," said Maurice.

"Oh. Okay."

The men turned and Reginald started to follow them, but then Penelope put a hand on his shoulder and turned him around. He looked into her eyes and found himself becoming lightheaded. She smiled and stroked his cheek. Reginald found himself repeating a foreign thought that seemed to have been borrowed from the lips of Todd Walker: *I could nail her.*

"Come on," said Maurice, grabbing Reginald's other shoulder. And so Reginald did, but before his eyes left Penelope, she mouthed the words, *We'll miss you.*

They walked through the lobby of the bowling alley and down the back hallway, went through a door, and emerged into a rear parking lot. The main entrance was at the front, and most of the cars were parked there. There were only four cars and two dumpsters behind the building. The lot felt cavernous and quiet.

Maurice put a hand on Reginald's chest and looked in his eyes. Then, very authoritatively, very unlike the shy and quiet IT professional Reginald knew from the office, he said, "Stay here. You won't be interested in our discussion."

Reginald decided to stay where he was. He leaned sideways against a dumpster, his elbow on the lid. He discovered that he wasn't remotely interested in what the three men were going to talk about. He was mostly interested in staying where he was. In fact, he couldn't conceive of *not* staying right where he was. Once Maurice said it, it seemed so obvious.

Despite his intense interest in staying by the dumpster and his relative lack of interest in what Maurice, Charles, and Isaac were doing, Reginald caught the gist of their conversation. Charles and Isaac had apparently been sent to reprimand Maurice about something that was, naturally, far less interesting than standing by a dumpster.

Charles even pulled a sheaf of official-looking papers from an inside pocket of his coat and tried to give them to Maurice in the way a server would hand over a summons, but Maurice slapped them away and laughed. There was some shouting. Reginald heard a few uninteresting phrases and snippets tossed around. Among them were Charles saying, "Your age doesn't give you any authority" and "Relic of a obsolete era" (despite being uninteresting, that caught Reginald's attention because it was such a strange thing to say) and Maurice saying something about "bigotry" and "short-term thinking" and about his "not recognizing authority" of some kind. It was all very uninteresting.

Suddenly there was a sensation on his ear that cut through his lack of interest like a knife. There was a puff of cold breath on his neck. A soft, sexy voice at his right shoulder purred, "We couldn't stand to be away from you."

Over the other shoulder, on the dumpster side, another voice and another cold breath: "You're... *intoxicating.*"

Right: "We were *supposed* to stay inside, but..." And a giggle.

Left: "It's *fun* to be naughty."

He turned and found himself face-to-face with Moira. Her face was two inches from his. She smelled amazing. She was unbelievably pale. He found himself falling into her green eyes, which had a silver tinge, as he'd fallen into Penelope's earlier. They were the most beautiful things he'd ever seen.

"Do you want to be *ours*?" she said.

"*Ours*," purred Penelope's voice somewhere to his side.

"You don't have to choose between us," said Moira.

"We can share," said Penelope.

"Yours," said Reginald.

He fell and fell and fell into her eyes, and then there was a distant pain and then nothing at all except pleasure, and everything he'd ever, ever wanted.

# FIGHT FIGHT FIGHT

IN HIS MEMORY, THE SCREAM he makes is an exclamation of pleasure rather than an expression of pain. Moira is on one side and Penelope is on the other, their mouths and tongues soft and sensual on his neck. The feeling is like being between two erotic clouds. He feels himself floating, careless of matters that seemed so pressing just a few hours earlier. But despite this, despite his ecstasy, Maurice reacts in anger as if it's his business to deprive Reginald of his companions. It happens like magic, the back of Maurice's head suddenly becoming his irate face as he hears the scream, as if he'd turned it faster than the eye could see.

In the next moment, the women fly backward as Maurice appears in front of him, both Penelope and Moira landing on the pavement near the back door to the bowling alley. Reginald feels his euphoria lift and pain descends like a hammer, his head feeling as if it's been mostly severed at the neck. But moments later, blessedly, the pain starts to dissolve into a swimmy semiconsciousness and he feels his shirt becoming wet, starting to sit heavy against his skin.

His perspective changes and he wonders why, but then realizes that he's fallen against the dumpster and has slumped down, and might have been that way all along. He's not sure. The world is nothing but pain and obscene fantasy.

*Exhibit:* Maurice yelling like some kind of a beast, a roar coming from him that can't be made by a man.

*Exhibit:* The two women skittering backward on their hands and feet, chests up, moving like crabs.

*Exhibit:* Maurice rounding on Isaac and Charles, returning to where they're standing so fast that Reginald knows he must have lost a blink of consciousness, and Reginald is suddenly very interested in going to sleep as soon as this odd dream ends. Anger radiates from Maurice like heat from a coal, somehow blaming the men for whatever has gone wrong, and suddenly the fact that Maurice is very much in charge is apparent to everyone. Isaac and Charles back away. Maurice says something. Isaac says something back and, fear and anger mixing on his face, pushes Maurice in the chest. This is the wrong thing to do. Maurice pushes back, but it's more like a *strike* than a *push* and the noise is like a sledgehammer hitting a steak and suddenly where Isaac was is not where Isaac is and he's flying backward across the parking lot, striking a car, the car folding in half around him, broadside, the car/Isaac hybrid then flying into a lamppost, which falls over in a shower of sparks.

Maurice is suddenly back by Reginald in another quick cut of memory, too fast to have actually happened, and then Penelope appears — doesn't climb onto, but *appears on* — Maurice's back. Both of Maurice's hands swing over his head and behind his back and then he's got her lengthwise and then, as if she were a twig, he brings her down onto the top of the second dumpster, on the other side of the back door. The dumpster, humbled by the impact, warps at the front edge and its right front wheel digs two inches into the concrete with a sound like a shotgun.

And then Isaac, who is obviously dead, appears in front of Maurice, clearly not just *not dead* but also *unhurt*. And now *he's* angry, and who could blame him after being blown into a car and then into a lamppost, and his hands go to Maurice's throat and his teeth bare and they're sharp and his fingers are like claws, tendons twitching in his forearms, but then he stops suddenly, backing away, his hands up like a supplicant.

There's a blur as Maurice's arm moves at his waist, and Isaac disintegrates into fire, like the flash of a pile of gunpowder.

Then Maurice is over Reginald, ten or twenty feet tall, his coat pendulous behind him like a cape and Charles, Moira, and Penelope are making odd noises of surrender, their hands up and palms out, backing away, and Charles is on one knee and there are sparks from the felled lamppost and shouts and then

# FOG

MAURICE'S FACE IS ABOVE REGINALD'S. The terrible thing that Maurice became a minute ago or a second ago or a year ago is gone and this is now just Maurice again, and Reginald wonders why he's laying on the floor somewhere, he doesn't know where. He remembers furor and fire and as he starts to fall asleep he asks the most irrelevant but most interesting question on his mind.

"What happened to Isaac?" he croaks.

"My sword," says Maurice. "It's tipped with wood."

This is as good of an answer as any, and Reginald lets sleep take him again.

# DRINK

SOMETHING WET IS AGAINST REGINALD'S mouth and he wonders if it's water. Then there's movement and he remembers that it's Maurice there with him, somewhere, and possibly they're bowling. Maurice's arm is hurt; it's red with blood and Reginald wonders if he can still pick up that spare, if the pizza Reginald ordered is ready yet.

"Stay here," says Maurice. "Look at me. Look."

So Reginald finds Maurice's eyes and suddenly, as he peers into them, there is a modicum of clarity.

"I can make you focus and I can make you decide, but the actual decision has to be yours," says Maurice. And the bloody arm is above him and Reginald wants to wince, but can't summon the will.

"Decide?" says Reginald.

"Decide to die now, a few minutes early," says Maurice, "so that I can save you."

"Sure," says Reginald, and then Maurice covers his mouth with the arm, trying to smother him, and despite the smothering he can feel the blood running down his throat and then a great pain climbs his spine, starting from the base and radiating through every nerve and it's like being

consumed by fire while being slit open by a
thousand razors and there's a great flash of light
and

# DEAD

REGINALD AWOKE PAIN-FREE, FEELING good, feeling strong. He didn't know where he was or how he'd gotten to wherever he was, but one thing he knew was that he was sitting in a pool of red liquid so large that it had to be some sort of gross practical joke.

"What is this?" he asked Maurice, holding up a dripping red hand and spreading his fingers. Something seemed to be wrong with his eyes. The liquid appeared pearlescent, as if lit from within.

"It's blood," said Maurice, who was sitting on a rock a few feet from Reginald and looking off into the distance. He turned to Reginald. "*Your* blood."

"It can't be my blood," said Reginald. "There's gallons. I'd be dead."

Maurice turned to look forward again. "Yeah, you would be."

Reginald looked around himself. "This is disgusting."

"You should have seen it before," said Maurice. "Wait until the police find the puddle behind the bowling alley. It's much bigger than this one."

Reginald looked down. He was on a concrete pad at the top of a hill. There was nobody around. It looked like it might be an observation patch used by hikers who came up through the woods, but if that were the case, then the police would be alerted to a second large puddle of blood when the hikers came through. Quite the busy night.

"You brought me up here?"

"Couldn't stay at the bowling alley. Too much noise. People were coming."

"Where are we?"

"The park. The big one." He pointed. "That's I-17 down there."

Reginald wondered why he wasn't woozy, especially if he'd lost as much blood as Maurice had said he had. But he *wasn't* woozy. In fact, he felt sharp and clear-headed. He did the calculation in his head.

"The park is an hour from the bowling alley by car. And you didn't have a car."

"I ran. Carrying you."

"What time is it?"

"Eleven thirty."

"You're missing work," said Reginald.

"Yes," said Maurice. "But it's allowed. I'm on paternity leave."

Reginald didn't understand that, but it was no more bizarre than claiming to have run forty miles with a three hundred and fifty pound load in an hour, so he let it go.

Reginald strolled away from Maurice, taking in his surroundings. He'd never been up this far, but he realized that knew where he was. He knew there was a trailhead a bit farther down the hill, near a picnic area that was reachable by car. His mother had taken him to that picnic area a dozen times throughout his childhood and into his adulthood. No, wait. Fourteen times. The last time had been on April 28th. He remembered that very clearly.

There was a square post in the ground twenty or thirty feet away. Reginald walked over and touched it. There was a blue metal arrow nailed to the post, and the arrow pointed to a gap in the woods. Reginald reached back in his memory until he could see the other end of the blue trail near the picnic ground in his mind. That end of the trail left the area almost vertically. Impossible to climb without getting down on your hands, in fact.

He marched back to where Maurice was sitting. Reginald realized that he could see a webbing of veins in Maurice's face and neck, and on his hands. He wondered why he hadn't noticed it before, because it looked sickly. Perhaps painful. He gasped.

"You've noticed the change in your vision," said Maurice.

"Did I hit my head?"

"No. This is something else. Tell me, can you read that billboard down there?"

Reginald looked where Maurice was pointing and was able to make out a yellow billboard with an advertisement for a lawyer on it. He read the words on it aloud to Maurice, then gasped. It had been easy and natural to read it, but now that he looked again, he realized that the billboard was only an inch across in his field of vision. He could hold his arm at full length in front of him and the billboard wasn't much larger than his fingernail. It had to be miles away.

"Sorry," said Maurice. "I meant that one." He pointed again. "To the left."

"Which?"

"The blue one."

"I don't see a blue one."

"Almost directly to the left of the one you just read, then higher up."

Reginald squinted into the distance. He could see a blue speck, but nothing that looked much like a billboard. Nothing within reason, anyway.

"All I see is that blue speck above the two red lights, near the horizon."

"Yes. That one."

It was easily ten times as far away as the yellow billboard. He couldn't even tell that it *was* a billboard, let alone read it.

"Of course I can't read it," he said. "It has to be ten miles away."

"Probably about fifteen," said Maurice, standing. "From this height, the horizon is nearly twenty miles off. I can see a sign on top of a gun store near Harvest Street, which has to be fifteen miles at least. I could read farther, but the curvature of the earth prevents it."

Reginald decided to let that go too. Too much was odd right now, and he decided he should pick his battles carefully. So he asked something more pertinent.

"How did I really get up here?" he said.

"I told you. I carried you."

"I weigh almost three hundred and fifty pounds," said Reginald. "And that trail back there? It comes out of the lower trailhead at a forty-five degree angle."

Maurice walked over to Reginald and wrapped an arm around his legs. Before Reginald could protest, Maurice lifted him in the crook of one arm as easily as Reginald lifted his 2-year-old niece. Then he set him down without comment.

"What are you, some kind of circus strongman?"

"Oh, come on, Reginald," said Maurice, suddenly looking nothing like his usual, young goth self. He looked older. In fact, he looked almost amused. "Stop being so obtuse. You saw what you saw, if you'd let yourself believe it. I'm a vampire, and now so are you. You've figured that out by now."

"Ha ha."

Maurice opened his mouth in a sharp, fast motion. Fangs descended from his upper incisors.

"Neat," said Reginald.

"You have them too."

Reginald felt his teeth. No, he didn't. Then something happened and suddenly he did. They had descended somehow, spearing his finger and drawing blood.

"This is always the lamest part of any supernatural story, where the person refuses to believe it all," said Maurice. "I'd love it if we could skip the drama."

Reginald, strangely unafraid, thought about the proposition in front of him. It made sense. Supernatural feats. Fangs. Blood. He'd seen the movies. Part of him wanted to protest and recoil, but another part — a part that felt new, and making itself at home inside of his head — told him to man up and be the first person ever to see what was right in front of his eyes. His new, vampire eyes.

"Okay," said Reginald.

"You're on board?" said Maurice.

"Yeah, sure. Why not?"

"You understand that you're done with daylight. You can only be out at night, or you'll need to stay inside all the time. You'll need to call into work and change your shift so that you're working at night, like me. And if they won't change you over, you'll need to find a new job."

"No problem," said Reginald. He wasn't big on natural light anyway, and this would get him away from Walker and his clones. Win freakin' win.

"You'll never age."

"Good deal."

"You'll never die unless you get staked or get stranded in the sun. Or unless you go tanning. No tanning, Reginald."

"No problem."

"And you'll need to drink blood to live, of course."

That was gross but not in the least unexpected. He'd already thought about it, and he guessed he'd get used to it.

"Can I still eat pizza?" he asked.

Eventually Maurice said, "I guess."

Then something struck him, and what struck him made him suddenly excited.

"Wait," he said, holding a finger up to Maurice. "Check this out."

He turned back toward the blue trail and, new vampire nature running through his veins and nerves, ran as fast as he could. The trees blurred around him. He felt wind against his face. His arms pumped. His legs thundered. He wasn't tired. He felt exhilarated, the world seeming to swim by as if in a dream, the horizon rotating like a record on a platter, and then it rotated end for end, the ground above and then the air above, and again and again and again until his face hit a rock and he heard his nose break.

He rolled over onto his back, panting, his breath trying to climb out of his chest. Then his stomach clenched and he rolled to the side just as he exploded into fits of vomiting.

The last thing he saw before blacking out was blood — probably Maurice's blood — in a pool of something that looked like oatmeal.

# FALLING SHORT

HE AWOKE ON THE SLAB again, feeling deja vu. Only this time, he was clear of the giant pool of congealing blood and his chest was moving up and down, up and down. He was sweating, and he barely had control of his breath. Maurice was standing over him.

"Don't try that again," said Maurice.

"What the hell?" said Reginald. "I'm breathing. I'm sweating. I'm supposed to be dead."

"Let me ask you something," said Maurice. "In vampire movies, do the vampires bleed?"

"Sure."

"How is that possible, if their hearts don't work?"

Maurice sank down into a squat at Reginald's side.

"How about changes in hair? With the exception of *Interview with the Vampire,* we've never seen a vampire who can't change his or her hairstyle, grow it longer, grow a goatee. What do you make of that?"

Reginald didn't see what Maurice was getting at.

"One more. In those same movies, how do vampires get their nutrition?"

"They drink blood," Reginald answered.

"How would that work, if their digestive systems don't function?"

Reginald sat up, his senses returning. He used his sleeve to mop what had to be a half cup of sweat from his forehead and neck.

"What are you trying to tell me?" he said.

Maurice sat down next to him, sighed, and said, "The agent that makes us vampires changes us, Reginald. It changes our eyes, our ears, our brains, our nerves, our blood. It alters the function of all of our organs and all of our systems. It makes our muscles work better. We get stronger. It makes us more or less impervious to the things that used to kill us, save sunlight and penetration of the heart by wood. And perhaps most importantly, vampirism allows us to heal amazingly fast. But what you need to understand is that *all of those organs still function.* We can run fast because our muscles heal as fast as we damage them. Our cells heal faster than we can deprive them of oxygen. We can be shot and stabbed through the lungs *not* because we don't need to breathe, but because we can heal the damage instantly."

"Is this just... you know... FYI?" said Reginald.

"Becoming a vampire means, more than anything, that you'll heal instantly, with emphasis on the idea that 'heal' means *'to return to your previous state.'* You could cut off my leg and it'd grow back. But..." He rolled up one of his pantlegs and pointed at a white line just above his ankle. "But this scar? Watch."

Maurice pulled a small knife from his pocket. It was very sharp; Reginald could see the uneven, ugly wear that suggested it had been repeatedly sharpened beyond the pristine and pretty edge it'd had when it left the factory. Maurice hesitated half a beat, then sliced the blade into the skin above his ankle. He inhaled with a hiss. Then, with one quick motion, he sliced away a chunk of skin as thick as a swatch of leather. Blood spilled to the dirt.

Then, within seconds, the wound became pink and then pale. Hairs sprouted. And as the skin knitted, the scar reappeared.

"Reginald," said Maurice, "are you familiar with the process that goes into determining whether a person will be granted a sex change?"

As much as Reginald didn't know where Maurice was going before, he really didn't know where he was going now.

"Noooo..."

"It's not just a medical procedure. Prospects are required to go through rounds of therapy and counseling and hormone treatments... all with the purpose of *making sure they truly want to commit to an irreversible change, and of preparing them for that change.*"

"Are you saying..."

"I don't know that I should have turned you," said Maurice. "It was an impulse, and it was rash. Maybe too rash. *Probably* too rash, actually.

You're ill-equipped. You didn't know what you were getting into, and you didn't have time to prepare. I'm sorry, Reginald. I made snap decision. For some reason, I didn't just want to let you die."

"Um... thanks?"

"You may not be thanking me later. See, you're now more powerful than you've ever been, but a vampire's enhancement is always relative to their condition at the time of their change. I was fast when I was turned, and vampirism made me much, much faster. I wasn't particularly strong, but I did get stronger, and I developed more strength with age. You, on the other hand..."

"I'm a fat vampire."

Maurice shrugged. "Did you ever wonder why there are no legends about overweight vampires? It's not because vampirism makes you fit. It's because just like with a sex change, becoming a vampire is usually something that a person enters into willingly. It's something that prospects know about well in advance — and because they know they're committing to never, ever changing, it's something people train for. It's like picking your hairstyle and wardrobe for a photo that will last forever. Before people become vampires, they get strong. They get fast. They get healthy. You wouldn't believe how many vampires are vegans and vegetarians before they're turned. It's ironic."

Reginald felt as if a great weight had settled on his shoulders.

"You, on the other hand, didn't have time to get prepared, either physically or psychologically. One day you were a human and the next day you are a vampire. You're going to find yourself at a significant disadvantage in the vampire community — especially today."

"Especially today?"

"Everything evolves with time, and the Vampire Nation is no different. I remember when the rules and practices surrounding creation were different, but..."

After Maurice trailed off, Reginald decided he should say something optimistic to lighten the dour mood.

"I wasn't much of a daylight kind of person anyway," said Reginald. "And now I can... wait. Let me try." Reginald rolled onto his stomach and did a pushup. "See? That's awesome."

"I don't think you respect the gravity of the situation," said Maurice.

"It's okay. I'll work on it. I'll be the fastest, strongest protege you've ever had."

"You aren't hearing me," said Maurice. "You *can't* train. You *can't* lose weight. A potential vampire usually takes three to six months to get strong, get lean, get fast, and get healthy. Nowadays, they train for sprinting and for combat. Muscle memory is physiological, so if you learn kung fu and then become a vampire, you'll be able to do it well forever. Every generation, people manage to get more and more physically refined before they take the blood, and they become amazingly powerful when they're turned. You, on the other hand, are untrained. The muscles and organs and systems you have now are as changed as they will be, ever again, for all of eternity. I'm sorry, Reginald, but you are exceptionally out of shape as far as vampires are concerned, and that will never change."

Reginald, who had grave doubts about the self-improvement field but who held a secret hope that Tony Robbins might someday come to magically save him, found this incredibly depressing. All of his life, do-gooders had been telling him that he could do anything he set out to do, that a person's potential was unlimited, that there was a fully realized version of himself deep inside just waiting to come out. And now he was being told that no matter what he did, he was screwed. It was as if Tony Robbins had walked into his house and punched him hard in the balls.

"'Whether you believe you can or you believe you can't, you're right,'" Reginald mumbled under his breath.

"Not anymore," said Maurice.

# BAKED

REGINALD TRIED TO CALL OFF work the next day. He was unsuccessful.

He phoned the office and asked the secretary to transfer him to Phil Berger. Phil was nearly identical to Todd Walker, and Reginald often confused one for the other if one of them went by too quickly. The only real difference between them was that Phil, who was his boss, seldom body-checked him into the walls when they passed each other in the hallways. Seldom, but not never.

"I can't come into work today," Reginald told him. "I'm sick."

"Can't give you the day off, Reggie," said Berger. "Try to be here in a half hour."

"I can barely stand."

"Twenty minutes if you can swing it. The fiscal year-end is coming and those spreadsheets won't fill themselves in."

Reginald sighed as he hung up. He was bone tired. Sitting through work — on zero sleep and up while the sun was out — was not going to be easy.

After their sobering heart-to-heart on the hill the night before, Maurice had led Reginald down the blue path, past the trailhead, all the way to the base of the big hill. Then, once they were back on flat ground, Reginald told Maurice that he wanted to test his legs again. Maurice advised him to dial his speed back and told him that being a vampire was like running an engine without a governor. Although his body would allow him to push very hard for a long time, doing so would burn him out — whereas a somewhat slower but still very fast speed (something Maurice called his "sustainable top speed," the speed at which his body would be able to repair itself as fast as he damaged it) would keep him upright, and keep him from running out of steam.

While Reginald experimented with faster and slower running speeds, Maurice added that whatever his top speed was now, it would change. He'd get faster as he got older, for one, and he'd get an extra infusion of speed and stamina once he fed for the first time. For the first few days, however, Reginald was kind of like a vampire in reverse. His new nature was actually feeding on what remained of his human blood, and that would provide him with enough sustenance for three or four days. After that, he'd start to get hungry and weak, and he'd need to learn to feed himself.

Then Maurice told him that blood had a kind of telepathy, and that the two of them were bonded by blood for as long as they both lived. Because of this, Maurice said that as Maurice's vampire nature fed itself inside of Reginald's body, he could actually taste Reginald as if he were feeding on him himself. This seemed embarrassingly intimate to Reginald, so he said nothing.

A minute later, he noticed how Maurice kept grabbing his side while they were running.

"What's wrong?" Reginald asked.

"Side stitch. And nausea," said Maurice.

"Vampires get nausea?"

"Depends on what we eat," he said. "I'm considered a health nut amongst vampires. I usually feed only on vegetarians."

"What have you been eating that's got you sick?" Reginald asked.

Maurice took a breath and held it as if fighting through a cramp. "You," he said.

"Oh," said Reginald. "Sorry."

"No problem," said Maurice. Then he turned and vomited on the side of the road.

Reginald's sustainable top speed turned out to be, unsurprisingly, far slower than Maurice's. Even with Maurice incapacitated, he kept having to stop and wait for Reginald to catch up. But that was okay. Maurice had said that older vampires were faster than young vampires and that he himself was quite old. He'd said that Reginald himself would improve with age, and might even improve some after feeding. And regardless of how much faster Maurice was, Reginald himself *was* fast and running was suddenly *easy*. He'd never run even a mile before, and so far they'd run several. He'd never felt so much wind in his hair. He felt invincible. He wished a car would go by so that he could race it. He wanted to see if he could catch a deer on foot.

"This is amazing!" he said to Maurice.

Maurice, at his side, smiled.

"I could run a marathon!" he said. "In no time at all!"

"Good for you," said Maurice.

"I'm not tired! I feel so energized!"

"That's fantastic."

"Fuck out the way!" said a voice, and two teens on low-rider bicycles passed Reginald on the left. They slowly pulled ahead until they'd vanished in the distance, laughing.

After a few more miles, Maurice pulled a cell phone out of his pocket and called for a cab, and a half hour later Reginald was at home.

He tried and failed at sleeping for a few hours, but it was like sleeping in the middle of the day, which he'd never been able to do. Eventually he pulled himself out of bed bone-tired, wondering if his new vampire nature was asserting itself as a flipped circadian rhythm. He wondered if being awake during the day would drain him in some way, but Maurice hadn't said anything about that, so he figured it'd be okay.

Okay, but *really damn tiring*.

By the time he'd showered (scrubbing hard to remove all of the dried blood), shaved (he cut himself once and it healed instantly), and dressed (which was slow due to torpid fingers and the fact that he fell asleep while buttoning his shirt), it was after eight and well beyond his normal start time. He'd have to stay later, getting maximal doses of Walker. And...

Reginald stopped in his tracks and said, "Dammit."

Maurice had told him that being a vampire wasn't complicated. There were really only two things he needed to know to get through his first day, and then Maurice would meet him in the evening to work through the rest. One of those things involved feeding: he didn't yet need blood, and although he could eat human food if he wanted, he in no way needed it.

The other was a stern admonition to stay as far out of the sun as possible.

"Damn damn damn," Reginald said again, peeling aside a drape and looking out at his sun-drenched lawn.

What Maurice hadn't told him was whether he had to stay inside when it was sunny or if he could just avoid direct sunlight, perhaps even venturing out when it was overcast or while wearing sunscreen. Then he remembered what Walker had said about Maurice walking home in the mornings holding an umbrella and wearing long sleeves and gloves and decided that he could no doubt do something similar. And besides, he didn't have much choice at this point. An hour had passed since he'd talked to Berger.

So, Reginald donned a size 4-XL long-sleeved Oregon State hoodie that his mother had given him for Christmas last year and a pair of heavy gardening gloves. The gloves were the only ones he could find that were large enough for his hands. He found them in the garage. They had belonged to the house's previous owner and were pink with flowers on them. Reginald made a mental note to keep his hands in the front pocket of the hoodie until he got inside the office, and then to stow them post haste. That's all he needed to give Walker more ammunition.

Properly attired, Reginald climbed into his car in the windowless darkness of the garage. Then he whispered a little prayer of hope and opened the garage door. A shaft of yellow penetrated the gloom. Then, holding his breath and squinting against the exceedingly bright light, he backed out of the driveway.

Tires crunched on gravel as he backed into the street.

The sun even *seemed* dangerous as he made his way down the street. Something in his blood seemed to fear it. It made him nervous to be so totally surrounded by brightness. It was as if he were on a tiny lifeboat, surrounded by sharks. He'd have to ask Berger for a switch to the night shift immediately. There was no reason he couldn't switch. His work was only vaguely time sensitive, he didn't interact with any of his co-workers, and the company, as evidenced by Maurice, already had people working nights.

Reginald reached the end of the street. He put on his blinker and turned left, toward the office...

... and felt his face suddenly on fire, as if he'd taken a desk nap in a bed of red hot coals. His skin bubbled and boiled, and he heard himself start to scream. He could feel his cheeks sagging, melting, becoming liquid. His vision blurred and then became a flat, featureless black. He could feel the gelatinous content of his eye sockets run out and begin inchworming down his cheeks like a Slinky. His scream had started to disintegrate into a wet, gargling sound.

He was going to die right here. Day one and already out of the game. Someone would find his car with a pool of flesh and blood in the driver's seat, or maybe just ash, a huge hoodie and slacks and shoes in the middle of it all, and a pair of pink gardening gloves...

*Turn your head.*

But of course. The sun was still low in the sky, and he'd just turned to the east. It hadn't been bothering him a minute ago.

Reginald turned his head to the right and the boiling, melting sensation abated.

He took a deep breath, just trying to hang on. Two breaths. Three.

The burning diminished more and more, and then it was gone.

Reginald's hands traced his face with his gloved hands. Everything seemed to be back where it was supposed to be. He also had sensation back in the skin of his face. He could feel the roughness of the gloves on his cheeks, his forehead, his lips, his chin.

He kept his head turned, feeling as if a very large gun had been placed against it.

He'd made most of the turn before the burning had started and so his car, idling, had driven into a brick mailbox. Smoke and an acrid odor had filled the car. He reached down, fighting the urge to retch, and found the gearshift by feel. He depressed the brake and pushed the transmission into reverse. He wouldn't be able to look behind him. He'd have to trust the passenger-side mirror, and if someone or something was behind him, then so be it.

He backed up in a quarter circle, back to the stop sign.

Then, slowly, he reversed his entire course, backing into his driveway. He closed the garage door, felt the darkness cover him like a comfortable blanket, and sighed.

He didn't want to go back out there, no way and no how.

But because he was a man who did what he was told, he fought down the fear and thought of Maurice and his walk home, and then he went inside, grabbed the largest umbrella he had, and ran to work, east, with the umbrella held in front of himself like a shield.

# WORK

WORK WAS A CAVALCADE OF humiliating situations.

For one, it took nearly an hour to run the five miles to his office, and when he arrived, Walker and several of his doppelgängers were waiting in the lobby, clapping. Walker had spotted him from his office, which had a west-facing window, and had taken a movie with his cell phone that he was showing to the gathering when Reginald arrived. Walker clapped Reginald on the back and said that while he was glad Reginald had decided to get in shape, he could use some form tips — for instance, don't run with an umbrella, because it adds wind resistance. And by the end of Reginald's first five minutes, Walker had ordered Reginald a pair of jogging shorts and a moisture-wicking shirt. Or at least he'd tried to, but then had apologized that they didn't seem to have shirts big enough, and ordered a parka instead.

Then, once Reginald was safely in his cubicle, he found that he couldn't stay awake. Three separate times before lunch, he woke up quite unexpectedly to find that he'd fallen asleep on his keyboard, his screen filled with a repeating string of random letters (and, in one apropos section, nothing but "zzzzzzz"). At one point a new email arrived from Todd Walker, and Reginald opened it to find a photo Walker had snapped of him asleep on the keyboard, a puddle of drool leaking onto the dark surface of the desk.

He'd also gotten chewed out by Berger for being so late, and for being so sweaty. "If you want to get in shape, that's great," he said, "but do it on your own time." Then he made an exaggerated face and waved a hand through the air. "And then take a shower." Reginald considered protesting, but then ran a hand through his hair and found it wet, found it standing up and resisting his efforts to smooth it, and noticed the giant wet stains on his shirt, across the front, sticking to his back, and actually dripping at the armpits.

At the end of the day, hoping his boss's animosity had cooled, Reginald walked into Berger's office and asked to be transferred to the night shift. Berger said no, that he needed Reginald around when the accountants and bankers were awake. Reginald protested. Berger held firm. Finally, Reginald told him that he had a rare family disease that had recently fully developed and that he was ultra-sensitive to sunlight. He even Googled for a segment he seemed to remember on a news magazine show about a girl who couldn't get any sunlight at all and showed it to Berger to prove that this was a real thing, but still Berger was skeptical.

"I don't believe you," he finally said. "Why now? Why today, suddenly, with no warning, when you were okay yesterday?"

Rash action was going to be required.

Reginald took a deep breath and placed his hand in a ray of sunlight streaming through the window and onto Berger's desk. Immediately, his skin began to turn red and blister. Reginald yanked the hand back, making noises of discomfort, and shoved the hand into his pocket so that Berger wouldn't see how quickly it healed. Berger looked shocked. Finally, he nodded.

"So it's a real threat to your health?"

"Absolutely," said Reginald, seeing the light at the end of the tunnel. "I could die."

"Okay, You can work ten PM to seven AM, starting Monday."

Reginald started to protest, but then decided that it was kind of absurd of him to expect Berger to invert everything overnight, and so he let it go.

# BIG BRAINS

IN ORDER TO AVOID THE daylight remaining before he could switch to the night shift, Reginald called in sick on Wednesday, and planned to do the same on Thursday and Friday. He called early, before Berger's secretary was in, and left a message on Berger's voicemail. Then he turned his phone off for the rest of the day.

Maurice came over on Tuesday night before heading to work. It was Reginald's first full night as a vampire. He had some questions about his new life, and he had a story to relate.

"Yeah," said Maurice when Reginald told him about the day's events. "Daylight's a bitch."

They were sitting in Reginald's house. Reginald was on the couch, semi-supine, and Maurice was in a La-Z-Boy with the foot support up, a cigarette burning in his hand. He said he'd picked up the habit back in France, well after becoming a vampire. No, it didn't make sense, he said, but vampires liked to be chic, and smoking in Paris cafes was the height of chic at the time.

"It isn't just daylight," said Reginald. "A lot's a bitch so far. I've got to be honest. I'm not seeing the upside."

"Well, you'll never die unless you burn in the sun or someone stakes you," said Maurice. "You'll never get old. And you're stronger."

"Yeah," said Reginald. "Watch this." He picked up an empty can of Mountain Dew, flourished it for Maurice, and crushed it.

"Stronger than you were, I mean," said Maurice.

Reginald rolled his eyes and opened a new can of Mountain Dew. It turned out that vampires could eat and drink human foods if they wanted to, and Reginald, always a comfort eater, still very much wanted to. He'd already eaten two buckets of fried chicken since dinner, and the remnants were still on his face. There was a Sara Lee coffee cake warming in the oven and the corpses of three Twinkies at his feet. At the rate depression was setting in, he'd bankrupt himself on Cheetos and Yoo-Hoo within a month.

"It'll get better," said Maurice. "Like I told you, we get stronger and faster as we get older."

"How quickly does that happen?"

"Pretty quick," said Maurice. "You'll notice a significant difference in a century or two."

"That's not fast," said Reginald.

"Measurable improvement even in a decade, then," said Maurice with the air of someone conferring a great favor.

Reginald sighed.

"Are you hungry?" asked Maurice.

"Starving. That's why I ordered the pizza."

"You understand that human food doesn't nourish you anymore, right?" said Maurice.

"It nourishes my soul."

Maurice sat up. "What I was asking was, are you hungry for *blood*? Because by tomorrow or Friday, you're going to need something other than carbs and grease."

"I'm hungry a lot. How can I tell the difference?"

"Well," said Maurice, "if you feel like you will die — and I mean literally *die* — if you don't get some sustenance soon, that's blood hunger."

"I feel that way now," said Reginald.

"No you don't. That's just old habits."

Reginald waved his arm dismissively, indicating that Maurice was of no use to him.

After a few minutes of silence, Maurice hopped up buoyantly, like an aerobics instructor. "C'mon," he said. "Stand up. I want to try something. Have you tried anything physical since last night? Maybe your wind is getting better."

Reginald shrugged.

"Do some jumping jacks," said Maurice.

Reginald did. After twenty, he was starting to pant and sweat.

"I did twenty!" he said, jubilant.

Maurice shook his head.

"I'm not improving? Am I hopeless?"

Maurice didn't answer. Instead, he propped his elbow on a stack of *TV Guide* magazines like he wanted to arm wrestle. "Let me see your guns," he said. Then, noticing the look on Reginald's face, he added, "I'll go very light. I just want to see where you're at."

Reginald hunkered down and put his palm in Maurice's palm, which made Maurice's hand look like that of a child mannequin by comparison. He set his elbow on the *TV Guides* and looked up.

"Ready?"

"I guess," said Reginald.

"Push."

"I am pushing."

"I mean, push as hard as you can."

"I am pushing as hard as I can," said Reginald.

Maurice sighed. "Okay, then try to resist me. I'm going to push really, really light. Okay?"

"Okay."

There was a loud snap and Reginald's wrist exploded in a mess of tendons and veins. It was as if someone had thrown spaghetti into the air. Blood sloshed down his arm, and a tiny gusher from the severed artery began squirting Maurice in the face.

Maurice tilted Reginald's hand, which was still attached by a flap, back up and into place. It healed instantly. He grabbed a greasy KFC napkin that Reginald had tossed onto the floor and began mopping his face with it.

"Sorry," he said. Then silence hung in the air.

After a few minutes in which Reginald thought Maurice might be deciding to kill him after all, Maurice looked up with something like hope.

"What about your mind?" he said. "Have you ever been tested?"

Reginald had been a mediocre student. High school had been miserable and he'd wanted only to survive it, to make it to the next day and the next day until it was over.

"I was average. I got mainly B's in school."

Maurice shook his head. "Not the same thing. Have you ever displayed high creative aptitude? Are you good with math? Music? Memory? Problem solving?"

Reginald shrugged, unsure.

"Think about it," said Maurice, "because vampirism enhances our true mental natures just as it enhances our physical natures. The only hitch is, the things that get enhanced in your head aren't always the things you were good at as a human. It's like vampirism reads your innate skills right off of your DNA — the potential you were born with. Many new vampires are surprised by what they find they can do. I have a friend who'd never played an instrument before, but learned to play drums as good as any human alive in an hour. He discovered it quite by accident, by playing Rock Band and then deciding to try the real thing." Maurice nodded at Reginald's video game console and his Rock Band guitar and drum set.

"Are you asking if I'm good at Rock Band?"

"Just looking under the hood. Have you played since last night?"

"No."

"Want to?"

Reginald wanted only to drink his Mountain Dew and wait for his pizza, and maybe spend some time hoping to die. Everything else felt pointless and futile.

"Nah."

"You might be surprised, Reginald. Seriously. I was thinking about this last night. Typically, vampires are very good either above the neck or below, but seldom both. It's as if there's only so much improvement to go around. Most vampires end up being strong and fast, but not much more mentally adept than humans. The most mentally gifted vampires I've ever known were those who aren't perfect physically. It's like vampirism goes to your brain when there's not much else for it to work with."

Reginald barely heard the point about mental adeptness. He'd heard something else.

"You've known vampires like me?"

Maurice rocked his head back and forth a little, unsure. Then he said, "Not like you, no."

"But you've known vampires who weren't physically perfect."

"In the past. Yes."

"In the past?"

"Times change. Things change, even for us."

"Do you still know them? Can I meet them?"

Maurice bit his lip. "No. There aren't many around nowadays."

"But the old ones. What happened to them?" He was rising from his chair, finally feeling excited, but Maurice didn't seem to share his excitement.

Instead of answering, Maurice changed the subject. "Do you know about glamouring?" he said. "Skill at glamouring usually goes with better mental adeptness."

"Glamour. You mean like putting on makeup?"

"I mean like making humans do what you want. It's like hypnosis. I thought everyone knew about that."

Reginald raised his eyebrows, intrigued. The idea of making people do his bidding was promising. He could make Walker come to work without pants. He could get Berger to give him a huge raise. He might be able to get hot women to have sex with him, or at least get them to undress in front of him.

"Can I try it on you?" he asked.

"Vampires can't be glamoured," said Maurice. "Try it next time you're around a human. Just *one* human to start. Just look them in the eyes and start talking, never breaking eye contact. Ask them to do something small, like snap their fingers, to see what effect you have. You're either going to have a gift for it or not, and if you do, you'll figure it out with practice."

Reginald nodded, encouraged.

Maurice looked Reginald over, from top to bottom and down again. Then he leaned back against Reginald's breakfast counter and crossed his arms.

"Okay," he said. "Reginald, you are easily the most out-of-shape vampire ever created. Which means..."

"Gee, thanks."

"Let me finish. Which means that if lack of physical gifts really does correlate with increased mental gifts, you might have some value to the Vampire Nation after all. As a culture, we've gotten dumber since my time. I can see it happening. It might be coincidence, or it might not be. Stand up."

Reginald stood.

"I'm above average by today's standards, but among vampires as a whole I'm not particularly mentally gifted," said Maurice. He grabbed a book at random from Reginald's ramshackle bookshelf and looked at it. Then he showed it to Reginald. It was Stephen King's *The Shining*.

"I've never read this," said Maurice. He opened the book, looked down at it, and then there was a blur and the riffle of pages, like shuffling a deck of cards, as the stack of pages moved from Maurice's right hand to his left. "Now I have. People say this guy doesn't end books well, but I didn't see that boiler explosion coming."

He tossed the book to Reginald, who caught it with both hands. "Now you do it," he said.

Maurice had read the book in under fifteen seconds. Reginald looked at the thing in his hand as if he'd never seen it before.

"That's what 'not particularly gifted' looks like?" he said.

"I'm just fast," he said, pulling out a new cigarette and lighting it. "'Fast' is muscular. Humor me and try it yourself."

Reginald raised a finger and prepared to open the cover, but just as he did, Maurice jumped as if he'd sat on something. "Oh, I just thought of something." He set the cigarette in an ashtray and pulled his cell phone from his pocket and held it up.

"You're going to take a picture of me reading?" said Reginald.

"A movie," said Maurice, a slight smile on his face. "Go ahead; I'm rolling."

Reginald looked back down at the book. "But I've read it before," he said.

"Not like this, you haven't," said Maurice. "Go."

Reginald opened the cover and thumbed to the first page of the first chapter. He read about Jack Torrence's impression of Stuart Ullman as an officious little prick.

He looked up. Maurice nodded.

Reginald read the first page, then the second. Maurice was probably getting bored, but out of the corner of his eye, Reginald could see him smirking behind his phone. He read more. Then more. After ten pages and probably twice as many minutes, he finally looked up and stared at Maurice. "Okay, this is ridiculous. How long do you really want to stand there while I plod through this?"

Maurice wordlessly held up the cigarette he'd lit before turning on the camera. Reginald could still see the square end in the ash from when the cigarette was new, meaning that it was burning very, very slowly.

Then Maurice gestured at the clock on Reginald's wall to show him that it had stopped at some point while Reginald had been immersed in operations at the Overlook Hotel.

Reginald shrugged, but something was strange. Maurice was smiling.

"What?"

"This is good," said Maurice.

"What's good?"

"How did that feel?"

"I don't know. Normal?"

"How long were you reading just now?"

Reginald shrugged. "Ten minutes?"

Then Maurice walked to where Reginald was standing and pressed a few buttons on his phone. Reginald saw himself on the small screen, staring down at the book.

The tiny Reginald on the phone said, "But I've read it before."

And offscreen, a closer, deeper voice said, "Not like this. Go."

The picture jarred slightly as, Reginald remembered, Maurice had nodded back at him.

Onscreen Reginald looked back down, and there was a blur of white at his fingertips. Then onscreen Reginald looked up and said, "Okay, this is ridiculous. How long do you really want to stand there while I plod through this?"

Reginald looked up, his mouth hanging open. Maurice was grinning.

"You know how they say that time flies when you're having fun? It's vastly magnified for vampires. When you're doing something you're good at, you fall into it and you lose track of time... if you choose to perceive it that way. Apparently you can be fast at a few things after all. Faster than me, even. Like I said, this is good."

Maurice pressed his lips together, smiling an appraising half-smile from half of his mouth. He seemed to be truly enjoying himself. He pocketed the phone, set the cigarette back in the ashtray without disturbing the squared-off end of the ash, and crossed his arms.

"Finish it," he told Reginald, pointing at the book still in his hand.

This time, now aware that he could apparently speed-read, the experience was different. It didn't precisely feel like it took him hours to read the book, but he *did* feel, somehow, as if he'd sat down with the story and the characters for a day, a week, maybe a month. It was as if the entire experience was suddenly sucked into his mind within the span of a few seconds, but then it dilated in his memory to a much longer period of time. He wasn't sure if he'd spent a long time reading, or a little.

Reginald looked up. The cigarette was still burning where Reginald had set it, still with the square end of ash stubbornly in place.

"How long did that take?" he said.

"Less time than I've ever seen," said Maurice. "Maybe I did a good thing, turning you."

Reginald didn't know what to say, so he bobbed his head in agreement.

"Now," said Maurice, taking the book from Reginald and opening the cover, "I have a question. What's the first word of the book?"

That was easy. He'd read it before. "Jack," he said.

Maurice nodded, then flipped to the back. "And the last word?"

"Sun."

"Okay," said Maurice, flipping to the middle, "time to take off the training wheels. What's the title of the 32nd section?"

Reginald didn't know how Maurice expected him to know something so obscure. The book was written in short chapters, and in the edition Reginald owned, the pages didn't even break between chapters. The chapter headings were like subheads, and there were a ton of them sewn right into the narrative of the story, and there was no way he

"'The Bedroom,'" he found himself saying.

His face must have registered surprise because Maurice chuckled and said, "This is like using a muscle on a limb you never knew you had," he said. "It's going to take some getting used to. Just trust yourself."

"But I didn't know it!" Reginald blurted.

"And yet," said Maurice with a Vanna White wave of his hand, "you did."

Reginald didn't know what to make of this odd new ability. Even now, he had no knowledge of the individual chapter headings. In any normal sense, he did *not* — even now — know the chapter title that Maurice had asked for. But then, he also kind of did. He could see a strange afterimage in his head, as if he were staring at the page. He closed his eyes, and without the conflicting sensory input, he almost *could* see the page. Right there: *32*, in italics. Below it, further to the right, none of it centered, THE BEDROOM, all in caps. The previous section ended with the word *now*. The first word of Chapter 32 was *Late*.

Maurice said, "What message does Halloran receive from Danny at the bottom of page 314?"

Reginald closed his eyes and it was as if he'd turned a page in his mind. He read the sentence at the bottom, all in caps, italicized, framed by parentheses.

"COME DICK PLEASE COME DICK PLEASE." Then, because he couldn't help himself, he added, "That's what she said."

"Which word is hyphenated at the end of the first line on page 215?"

Reginald closed his eyes and...

"Keep your eyes open," said Maurice. "It's not actually visual, so don't reinforce that idea for yourself. You want to be able to use this while being fully present wherever you are."

This time, the knowledge just arrived at his lips. It seemed to bypass both the visual image and his conscious awareness. "Canvas."

"The last word of chapter 33?"

"Danny."

"The eighth line from the bottom on the sixth complete page of the first section?"

"Was he a college graduate."

"You say that like a statement," said Maurice.

"The question mark is missing. It's a typo." Then, surprising himself, he added, "It was fixed by the 1992 mass-market paperback edition."

Where had that come from? One time, sitting uncomfortably in a tiny faux leather chair in a Barnes & Noble bookstore to kill time while his mother got her nails done at a salon in the mall, Reginald had picked up a copy of the book and had begun reading. That had to be ten years ago.

"Interesting," said Maurice. "Apparently it's not just new information. You have no idea how rare that is, to pull that kind of recall from the archives of your prior, unenhanced human brain."

Reginald nodded, surprised but pleased. "I've never been particularly smart," he said.

"Competent. Organized. But I never took any honors classes or anything like that."

Maurice closed the book and set it on the counter. "Tell me: What's the square root of sixty-five thousand, eight hundred and ninety-four?"

"Two hundred fifty-six point six-nine-eight... you get the drift."

Maurice picked up his cigarette and drew on it. "I'll have to take your word for that," he said, "that not being one of my abilities. You are going to be an exceptionally gifted glamourer. It all goes together. You'll be good at music, too, if you care to be. Music and math are very closely related."

"It feels like parlor tricks," said Reginald.

Maurice shook his head. "It's not. This isn't just recall. It's *function*." He locked eyes with Reginald, becoming serious. "And when, over the next weeks, you feel like you're not a very impressive vampire, I want you to remember something: At this, you are *exceptional*."

"Exceptional?"

"Like nothing I've seen before. You've got a bit of a secret weapon."

With this, Maurice stabbed the cigarette out in the ashtray and rose to his full height, which wasn't much. He was still wearing the sword on his belt, which Reginald thought ruined the otherwise suave image he'd displayed tonight. But the sword had its purposes, he guessed.

"Wait," said Reginald. "You're leaving?"

"I need to get to work."

"But..." Reginald whined, loathe to be alone with his odd new ability, "... you haven't taught me anything about how to be a vampire!"

"Stay out of the sun. Avoid wood stakes. Keep a low profile. Feed, but that comes later. And I'll be back tomorrow night, so don't worry."

"What about sleeping?"

"Do it. During the day."

"Do I need a coffin?"

"Only if you're morose."

"What about silver?"

"Silver is bad. It'll burn your skin and make you weak."

"What about...?" He couldn't think of anything else.

"Relax, Reginald. There's simply not that much to it, and there's no real training to be had. You're kind of like an animal now, and you'll find that your instincts have become much, much louder. The things you need to know will come to you naturally. Any details about any of it that you need, just ask."

Maurice pulled on his coat, and the doorbell rang. The pizza man.

"The pizza this guy brought you is just oral masturbation now," said Maurice, inclining his head toward the door. "But see if you can glamour him into giving it to you for free."

"How?"

"Look into his eyes. The rest is like what you did with the book. It'll come. Trust me."

The doorbell rang again. Maurice took a step toward the door.

"You're going to go out the same door he's coming in?"

"I'm fast. He won't see me."

"Wait!"

Maurice stopped, his hand on the knob.

"Um... how old are you, Maurice?"

Maurice shrugged. "Old enough. Let's just say that I knew Caesar."

Reginald, thinking of his pizza, said, "As in, 'Little'?" But the door was already open, the pizza man was pulling a box from the insulated bag he was carrying, and Maurice was gone.

# HUNGRY

ON THURSDAY, REGINALD SUCCESSFULLY SLEPT through most of the daylight hours. He woke up around six, ordered Chinese food, ate it while watching reruns on Fox, and then humiliated an entire box of Ho-Ho's he'd forgotten he had. It was nice to know he couldn't gain any more weight and that he wasn't begging for a heart attack or a diabetic leg amputation. So there were some upsides.

Maurice arrived around ten and apologized that he'd gotten a late start and didn't have much time to spend before heading to work. Then he asked how Reginald had done in his attempt to glamour the pizza man.

Reginald reported great success. After he'd gotten the pizza for free and was preparing to send the pizza man on his way, he had, on impulse, told the pizza guy to stick around and play The Sims. They'd ended up playing until an hour before sunrise.

"And did you feed on him?" Maurice asked.

"Oh," said Reginald. "No. Was I supposed to?"

"I thought you might. I didn't want to suggest it. I wanted to see if you felt it by instinct."

"I was pretty full from the pizza," Reginald explained. But then Maurice gave him that look again and he said nothing further.

"You'll need to feed tonight or tomorrow. It's time. Every few days at most from here on out. The bad news is that I don't have time to hunt with you tonight, but the good news is that you don't really need me to. And if for some reason you can't figure it out, you'll be fine until tomorrow and I can show you then. Good pickins on Friday nights. That's when the freaks come out."

"I'll wait."

"I'd rather you at least try on your own," said Maurice. "Maybe you've noticed how I keep trying to get you to learn things through instinct? There's a reason."

"I don't know..."

"You'll do fine," said Maurice. "Find someone alone somewhere and try it out. You'll know how to extend your fangs, where and how to bite, how to drink, and when to stop. This is stuff that is part of your biology now. Just don't forget to make *them* forget after it's over, assuming you don't kill them. And *don't*, by the way. Murder is so much harder to get away with now, and you're not ready to try."

Reginald had a disturbing moment wherein he realized that Maurice had certainly killed people, and probably a lot of them. In fact, he probably still did it today. But, Reginald told himself, saying his vampire friend killed was like saying that tigers killed. They did, but that's what tigers do.

"What if I terrify them? What if they scream?"

"Do it somewhere secluded. Use a gag if you have to. And when it's all over, don't feel guilty. You're going to make the bad memory go away, and they'll heal."

"Can't I just rob a blood bank?"

Maurice laughed. "If only. Everyone thinks of it, but it's too high-profile a crime. But you may get lucky someday and find someone who is willing to share their neck with you. Someone who wants you to feed on them."

"Sounds sick."

"Messed up humans are my bread and butter," said Maurice. "Look at me. You think I dressed like this in 17th century France? I'm a goth kid today because goths jump at the chance to be fed on."

"Really?" Reginald was trying to imagine himself as a goth. The visual was frightening. He'd look like a looming thundercloud.

Maurice nodded. "I've got to go. But try it. Go out and feed. Good luck."


After Maurice left, Reginald got in his car and procrastinated for an hour and a half, trying to submerge what he was beginning to suspect was blood hunger in a series of fast food errands. Everywhere he went, he sat in the car, snacking, watching people, trying to get a feel for how often they actually did walk solo, where, and *how* solo they'd need to be in order for him to feel comfortable chancing an attack.

Eventually he ended up at the waterfront. There was a path that ran along the river, and people walked the path at all hours. There were bars at one end and a residential area at the other end, so the path got crowded in the early evenings and again when the bars closed at 2am. Between those times, though, he hoped to find his virginal prey.

He sat on a park bench away from the path, in the shadows, and waited.

Some time later, he saw a woman coming toward him, jogging alone. Reginald thought that jogging alone at nearly midnight was a dumb thing for her to be doing, despite the widespread perception that the waterfront and the path — and, hell, downtown in general — was reasonably safe. A girl could get robbed doing something like that, or raped, or murdered. Or attacked by a vampire.

Reginald decided that what he was going to do to her would be far better than being raped or killed, considering he would make her forget all about it after it was over, and then send her on her way. It was the lesser of evils. He'd be doing her a favor, really.

She passed by without seeing him. Reginald took up pursuit from the rear.

With Reginald behind her in a jog, the woman approached a section of the path where two lights in a row had burned out, and the path was in shadows. This was his chance. Reginald moved faster. He wasn't going for a sustainable pace; this was a predator-and-prey situation. He sprinted. The distance closed. She'd never know what hit her. He could see a pair of white iPod earbuds in her ears, so she couldn't hear him. Perfect.

His lungs were beginning to burn and his heart was beginning to beat harder, but he fought down his fatigue. He told himself, rallying his new nature, *I am vampire!*

She was so close.

He reached a hand out, but the distance had stopped closing and had begun opening again. He watched as the space between his outstretched fingers and the jogger's back increased.

If he could just grab her jog top, he could pull her back and wrestle her to the ground. Then, once she was down, he could sit on her. It might not be dignified, but there were things he could do and things he couldn't, and he might as well play to his strengths.

But she was pulling away.

He summoned everything he had for one final push, his hand still out, his fangs descending, his blood crying out with lust...

... and then his lungs seized and his feet became heavy and he felt his bulk rolling forward, the pavement jumping up at him. He hit the ground hard with his face. His head rang. Then, finally still, his face to the blacktop, he breathed in.

Out.

In.

Out.

The world felt light and swimmy. An ant crossed an inch from his left eye carrying the shell of a sunflower seed. It seemed to stop and look at him with disgust, then move on.

He looked up without lifting his chin from the blacktop. He could see the woman further down on the path. She started to sing the refrain of whatever it was she was listening to, and a minute later she was gone.

"You okay, buddy?" said a voice.

Reginald rolled onto his back, his chest rapidly rising and falling. He felt like he was having a heart attack, except that was now impossible.

The speaker was an old man with a cane. Reginald wondered why he was out so late, then remembered that there was a senior apartment complex just behind them. The more capable among the residents could stroll to the waterfront, look around, and stroll back at any hour, especially given the safe neighborhood. Perfect for elderly insomnia.

"I'm very hungry," said Reginald.

"Can you get up? Come with me. I'll get you some food."

Reginald took several deep, shambling breaths. It was still hard to talk.

"Can I drink your blood?" he said.

"What?"

"Come down here. Look in my eyes."

"What's wrong with you, you sicko?"

"I need it. I need your blood." Two deep breaths. "Help me out here."

The man hit him hard in the ribcage with his cane and walked on, mumbling.

# TRYING AGAIN

ON FRIDAY NIGHT, FEELING MORE like a failure than ever, Reginald called Maurice and informed him that he was ready to begin learning to hunt. Maurice asked if he'd tried on Thursday as he'd suggested, and Reginald, unable to repeat his humiliating defeat at the hands of a jogger and a senior citizen to his vampire mentor, said he hadn't. Maurice sounded disappointed that Reginald hadn't even tried, but told him that the good news was that he could try tonight.

"With you. Of course."

"No," said Maurice. "Not with me."

Reginald thought he must have heard incorrectly.

"What do you mean, 'Not with me?'"

"I have to go out of town," Maurice told him.

"Wait. You're not coming over here at all?"

"I'm already on my way out of town. I'll be back Sunday."

Reginald couldn't believe what he was hearing. How could Maurice abandon him?

"Sunday? Are you kidding?"

"You'll be fine. Any vampire can feed. It's in your blood... no pun intended."

Reginald considered telling Maurice about last night's failure after all, but he couldn't bring himself to do it. It was too humiliating. Besides, if Maurice was really already on his way out of town, then there was nothing he could do anyway. Reginald's best bet was to act indignant. It wouldn't change anything, but at least it'd make him feel better.

"How can you abandon your prodigy on the eve of his inaugural feeding? I might die of starvation while you're off galavanting!"

When he replied, Maurice's tone was amused and not at all perturbed, but there was a seriousness in his voice that indicated that what he said was final... possibly even grave.

"This is an errand I can't refuse," he said. "Vampire Nation stuff. I'll tell you all about it when I get back. But in the meantime, you'll be fine. Even if you can't feed, you'll live. You may not *want* to live at that point, but you will." And he laughed, because he clearly thought this was a situation that would never come to pass. But after last night, Reginald thought it was a distinct possibility.

He begged for another minute or two and then hung up, thoroughly dispirited.

So it was off to the park again, then. How fun.

Before leaving, Reginald ran through his attack options in his head to find the scenario with the greatest likelihood of success. He'd need to wait for someone who was walking, not running. He'd need to approach with stealth, closing as much of the distance as he could before commencing the attack. It was a simple plan.

He planned in this way for six hours. Forming the plan took two minutes of that six hours, and the rest of the time was spent playing sudoku, which had gotten much easier in the past week. He completed three books, then spent some time imagining his inevitable failure. Then he got in the car and drove.

By the time he reached the waterfront, it was four-thirty — the time when the people who are up late give way to the people who are up early. Traffic on the path was very light.

It was a half hour before he saw his first group of people, and a while after that before he saw any singles. While he was waiting, sitting on his dark and lonely bench and wishing stupid Maurice hadn't taken his stupid self off on some stupid errand, he checked his cell phone. Sunrise was at 6:46. By the time he saw his victim, it was nearly five-fifteen.

The victim in question was a young man walking alone. He was texting. Like the woman last night, he had a pair of headphones in his ears. He wasn't paying any attention to the world around him.

Trotting up slowly, quietly, afraid to so much as breathe, Reginald came up behind the kid. With another night of hunger under his belt, he found that he could actually *smell* the young man's blood. It made his head spin. Maurice had been right. He *would* know what to do. He felt his fangs descend. The fangs seemed to have a mind of their own, and he could feel them pulling him toward living flesh. He knew, on some level, how the blood would taste. The thought didn't repulse him. It made him hungry. Only, it was more than hunger. It was a base, physiological *need*. The thought of feeding on the kid made his face burn. It was almost arousing.

His victim was wearing a brown hoodie, slung casually back. He was wearing a strappy undershirt underneath. His neck was tantalizingly exposed. Reginald got close enough to see the veins and arteries under his tan skin, throbbing and pulsing. Reginald's tongue licked his fangs, which didn't feel at all odd in his mouth. His breath became shallow, excited. He opened his mouth. Then he grabbed the kid with one hand on a shoulder and the other on the side of his head. Quickly, he leaned forward as if he were about to eat a watermelon.

The kid snapped away just as Reginald was about to pierce his skin, snatching the enticing neck away. He turned and stared hard into Reginald's eyes. Reginald was too shocked (and feeling the vampire equivalent of blue balls) to think of glamouring him. He just stood with his hands still in watermelon-holding position, his mouth open and his fangs out.

"What the *fuck,* homes?" said the kid. Then something changed in his face and he stared more closely at Reginald, who didn't know what to do and had frozen in place like a waxwork. His eyes were darting from side to side, waiting for someone to rescue him.

The kid said, "Are you a fucking *vampire*?"

Reginald nodded, slowly.

"I know you weren't about to drink *my* blood, motherfucker," he said, his face becoming angry.

Reginald decided to go for broke. He peeled his lips back and hissed. "I could break your neck before you knew what hit you. Make it easy on yourself and come back over here, and I'll let you live."

The kid shook his head. "I don't think so. The only thing you could break the neck of would be a bucket of fried chicken. Aren't you pretty fat for a vampire?"

"You don't know who you're messing with," said Reginald. "I own the night!"

"Dude, you don't own shit. You *should* own a treadmill." Then he laughed.

Reginald couldn't believe this. Even as a vampire, he was being mocked. He decided that if he concentrated all of his speed into one small motion, he could impress and scare the kid, to show him who was boss.

He pistoned his hand toward the kid's arm. The kid stepped back and slapped it away.

"Motherfucker! Get your hands off me! Fat faggot motherfucker trying to suck my blood. Knew I shouldn't have come out here tonight. Nothing but fat faggot vampires in the parks these days."

Reginald reached again, desperately hungry. He didn't have the energy or the time to try and find someone else, and he couldn't make it through another night. "Get over here," he said.

"Fuck off!"

"Come on. I'll be quick."

"Motherfucker, you *will* keep your hands the fuck off me!"

Reginald reached into his pocket and pulled out his wallet. "Tell you what. I'll pay you. I've got fifty bucks in here. Like, two minutes tops."

"The fuck is wrong with you, you fat fucking faggot?" said the kid, knocking Reginald's wallet out of his hand. "What kind of a vampire are you, paying people to let you bite them?"

"A hundred, then," said Reginald, stooping to pick up his wallet. "I only have the fifty, though, so you'll need to come with me to an ATM."

Then everything went black as the kid hit him, hard, across the chin.

He had a dream that he starved to death. He desiccated like a raisin and Maurice found him curled up in his house and said, "I knew I made a mistake." Then things in the dream changed and he was in hell, a vampire hell, with vampires everywhere, their legs and arms and hair on fire, forever in pain and forever burning but unable to die...

... and then his eyes opened and there was nothing but pain across his face as a beam of sunlight lanced him like a sword. He rolled away and it stopped, but a second later there was another pain in his hand, then on his face again. It was disorienting.

He fought the pain and got to his hands and knees and looked around. He was maybe ten feet off the path, more or less hidden from early-morning walkers by three trash cans marked for the disposal of aluminum, glass, and refuse. The sun was rising in the east, across the river, and he was mostly shadowed by a huge, overhanging tree. Sunlight was peeking through the shifting holes in the leaves, and each time one of the beams touched him, it was like being seared by a brand.

He scrambled back, deeper into the shadows.

As the sun began to rise, Reginald ducked back into the shadows under the tree. He figured he could spend the day on his usual bench near the trunk of a second, larger tree, but then he realized that he felt very hot despite the fact that his skin had already healed from the singeing.

He opened the buttons on his shirt. He rolled up his pantlegs and rolled down his socks. Then he took off the shoes and socks. If he'd had a razor, he would have shaved his head. Eventually, fighting embarrassment, he stripped off his shirt. His gut looked enormous and pasty in the outside air. But none of it helped, and sweat began to bead on his skin and pool in his belly button. It ran down his back and onto the bench, into his pants and underwear. His hair became a heavy, sloppy mess.

It was the sun.

Even though the shade was filtering out direct light, indirect light was bouncing off of every surface he could see. And really, that was just the visible spectrum. All of the other wavelengths of solar radiation were moving right through the leaves — right through the bark of the tree — and baking him.

As if to confirm this, his exposed white belly began to turn red before his eyes. He lifted one of the large folds of skin and found his flesh white underneath. He held the flap up and watched as the newly exposed skin began to turn red, too.

He had to get out of here. But to where?

*The bridge.*

There. Not far away, but far enough away to be terrifying.

As if playing a deadly serious game of "the floor is made of lava," Reginald slid off the bench and made his way across the grass, staying in the rapidly diminishing islands of shadow, until he reached the underside of the bridge over the river. He climbed up underneath it like a troll.

With several feet of concrete and rebar between him and the sun, Reginald began to cool down. He pulled his phone from his pocket. It was just after seven AM, and about fifty-nine degrees. He assessed his own temperature. Yes, that felt about right. He'd be safe here.

With no way to get home and nobody to call, Reginald settled in to spend the day under the bridge. There was one other person in the crook of the bridge with him — a homeless man who seemed very concerned that Reginald would try to steal his blanket. Reginald showed the man his fangs and the man took his blanket and ran. It was only after he'd left that Reginald realized he could have fed on the man, at which point Reginald told himself, yet again, that he was the worst, fattest, biggest failure of a vampire ever.

As the sun rose, he tried to sleep. It wasn't easy. There was no truly level surface up high under the bridge, and every time he tried to sleep, he found himself starting to roll down the incline and toward the jogging path. So he sat up and leaned against a stanchion, pulled out his phone, and watched YouTube videos until the battery had all but died. He decided to save a few minutes of usage just in case. Maybe he could get someone to deliver a pizza to a man under the bridge. You never knew.

A few hours later, several hot dog vendors set up within his line of sight. It was like torture. He didn't need hot dogs any more than he needed the pizza he'd ordered a few nights ago, but the memory of human hunger mingled with his blood hunger drove the sensation up to a fever pitch. He tried several times to get people on the jogging path to get him a hot dog, yelling at them from up under the supports, but each time he tried, the person he'd been trying to solicit either yelled obscenities at him or took off running.

By the time the sun set on Saturday, his hunger had become something physical. His skin, on his hands, was beginning to look dried and wrinkly. His stomach didn't rumble, but somehow his *blood* did. He could feel it in every part of his body, running outward from his core in long, ropy tendrils of desperation. With each heartbeat, need left his heart and screamed out in search of sustenance, and with each beat, blood returned to his heart empty-handed and sad. He could *feel* his blood's need in every cell of his body. What had Maurice said? It was like a limb he didn't know he had.

Yes, it felt like that.

Having been outrun by a woman, caned by an old man, and beaten up by a teenager, Reginald decided to lower his expectations. He wasn't ready for the big leagues. He had to go down past the farm leagues, past the minors, past little league. He needed the vampire hunting equivalent of preschool tee-ball.

So, as the sun was setting, he used the last of his phone's battery to do an internet search. After a few minutes of dead ends, he found a church that offered daycare for parents who worked late —

later than most daycares even on weekends, for later-than-normal parents.

This one would keep your kids until ten if necessary.

Past sunset.

# LITTLE GIRL

WHEN REGINALD ARRIVED AT THE church, the children were out in a well-lit, fenced-in play yard. There were quite a few of them. It seemed strange to Reginald that there were so many kids in childcare on a Saturday night, but apparently the church was the only game in town for parents who worked unconventional hours.

Reginald looked at his cell phone to check the time. It was eight-thirty. He sat on a bench a hundred or so yards from the play yard and, using his enhanced vampire sense of sight, watched and waited as over the course of the next hour, parents arrived and claimed their children. Reginald started to doubt his plan. How had he expected to ambush a kid while under the church's supervision or while holding their parents' hands?

Ten o'clock arrived. Reginald crossed his fingers. The lights went out. Someone opened, peeked out, and then locked the door to the play yard. Everything became quiet.

Ten minutes passed. Nothing.

Reginald swore.

He'd known this was a stupid idea. What had he expected? To grab one through the fence? To have one walk over and offer him- or herself up after the shop was closed for the night? The whole idea was stupid, and now that he thought about it, he realized he'd *wanted* it to fail. He couldn't bite a kid. He couldn't terrify an innocent child. And now he'd wasted almost two hours and the kids were all gone, but it was for the best, he'd just have to head back to the bridge and find that hobo, or head into the city and find a hooker with a bad enough drug habit to allow him to do something particularly kinky, or maybe he could...

The front door of the church opened and a small figure, wrapped in a jacket against the nighttime chill, emerged and began walking away.

Reginald watched for a few seconds. He could see a brown pony tail running down the back of the jacket. A girl. Judging by the height, he guessed she had to be nine or ten. Why was a little girl leaving the church as the daycare closed? Why was she left alone to walk the streets at night?

But in the end, it didn't matter. With his blood growling, hating himself for what he was about to do, Reginald got up and started to follow her.

The third time was bound to be the charm. Between the woman and the teenage kid, he'd learned exactly what not to do.

He approached the girl slowly, diving into pools of shadow behind her and keeping his footsteps light. There weren't many streetlights. The girl was wearing earmuffs. He doubted she'd be able to hear him.

Loathing rose in his throat. He pushed it down. She'd be fine. She'd be scared, and she'd be hurt, but afterward he'd make her forget and she'd continue on her way. He'd even follow her, he decided, to make sure she got home safely after he'd fed. He'd be energized. He'd want to return the favor.

And besides, he needed it. He really, really needed it. If he didn't feed soon, he'd die.

As if to confirm this thought, Reginald's leg hitched and he almost fell. A cramp curled his left hand into a claw. He looked down at his arm, at the claw hand, as it slowly relaxed. The skin on his arm was scaly and gray.

The girl would get over it. He needed the blood more than she did.

He sprinted toward the girl and grabbed her by both shoulders. Then, without hesitation, she spun as if she'd been waiting for this exact move, rotated ninety degrees, and slid sideways out of his grip. Then she ran.

He ran after her, feeling deja vu.

"Hey! Wait!" he shouted. He asked himself what a successful pedophile would say at this point and then yelled, "Your dad sent me to give you a ride home!"

The girl was running, but he was keeping pace just a few yards behind her. She wasn't screaming or panicking, but her running speed felt deceptively slow for someone her age. It was as if she was toying with him.

She turned her head and yelled back, "I've never met my dad!"

"I mean your mom!" Reginald huffed, already starting to lose his wind.

The girl didn't turn this time. Breathing easily, she said, "My mom would never do that!"

"I... I have candy!"

"Do you think I'm an idiot?" the girl yelled.

Reginald, already out of shape and further weakened by his need for blood, felt his legs give out as his breath fell short. He collapsed onto the ground and then, giving up, laid motionlessly on the concrete for the third time in as many nights.

Several minutes later, his heaving gasps for breath began to abate and he felt his pulse slow down. "I'm the worst vampire ever," he muttered aloud.

"You're a vampire?"

The voice wasn't far away. It sounded curious. Reginald lifted his face from the concrete and looked up. He felt a piece of gravel drop off of his forehead.

It was the girl. She was maybe twenty feet from him, standing under a streetlight. She was wearing a pink jacket with Hello Kitty on the front. The zipper bisected Hello Kitty, three whiskers on each side. A pair of fluffy white earmuffs were hanging loose around her neck. She must have removed them after their brief sprint.

"You're a vampire?" the girl repeated.

Reginald sighed. "Yes."

"But you're fat."

"Yes."

"I've never heard of a fat vampire."

Reginald rolled onto his back, then sat up. "There's a reason."

"Were you trying to eat me?" she asked. She didn't sound afraid, just interested.

"I'm sorry. I'm very hungry."

The girl shrugged. "Well, I'm not letting you do that."

Reginald sighed, then looked up. "Why are you still here?"

"I know I can outrun you," she said, her eyes avoiding his. He waited for her to say more, but apparently the subject was closed. Reginald rose to his feet and brushed the rest of the gravel and glass off of himself. The girl, true to her word, didn't move.

"I'm very hungry. And I'm a vampire," he said.

"I got that."

"I could just grab you before you could stop me. So you might as well just come over here and we'll make this easy."

"I don't think so," said the girl. "You're too fat."

"I was making it sporting," he said. But he could tell she wasn't buying it.

Reminding himself that his very survival was at stake, he lunged forward, determined to somehow move faster than he ever had before. He could do it.

But, no he couldn't. The girl turned and ran again, only this time she was laughing. Not in mockery, but like an elated child in the middle of some seriously great play.

They rounded a corner, then another, and then she sprinted up a set of steps to a small brownstone and  fumbled out a set of keys. She was going to open the door, and that would give him time to catch up...

... but it didn't, because Reginald was even worse at steps than he was at running. His belly bounced and struck his thighs as he climbed as if it were trying to drive him back down.

The girl was through the door before he reached the top of the stairs but he bounded after her, his hands out, and as she tried to close the door he threw his weight into it and it exploded inward. The girl stopped halfway down the inside hallway and looked back at him.

Feeling triumphant, he stepped across the threshold.

Then, he stepped across the threshold.

Then, he raised a foot and stepped across the threshold.

He looked down at his feet. Every time he placed a foot inside the house, an invisible force propelled it backward. With the repeated stepping and pushing out, it looked like he was doing the moonwalk.

And from inside, the girl said, "Cool." Then she walked forward, closed the door in Reginald's face, and locked it.

# FUCK THIS

WITH THE DOOR LOCKED AGAINST him, Reginald sat on the stoop and resolved to simply sit where he was until the sun rose. He'd burn, he'd die, and that would be the end of Maurice's little rash decision.

"Hey," said a voice from above. He looked up. It was the girl, her head and arms hanging out of an open second-floor window.

Reginald sighed.

"Hey," she repeated.

Reginald thought, *Go away. You've humiliated me, so let me catch my breath, and then I'll die.*

Something hit him on the head and bounced to the step at his feet. It was a button.

"Hey."

Another button hit his head.

"Hey."

And another.

He looked up. "What? What do you want?"

"What's your name?" she said. "My name's Claire."

"Reginald."

She frowned. "Do people call you Reggie?"

"They do. But I don't like it."

"Okay, Reginald," she said.

After a few seconds, she said, "What's it like, being a vampire?"

"It's not all it's cracked up to be."

"How did you get turned?"

But he didn't feel like small talk. Not in the least. He sighed and played with the buttons at his feet. Then he had an idea. He looked up. The girl was watching his feet too, watching him scoot the buttons around on the step below him.

"Hey," he said.

"Yeah?" Still looking at his feet.

"Hey."

"What?" Now looking at the top of his head.

"Look here," he said, pointing at his eyes.

"No."

"Just for a second."

She kept looking at the top of his head. "No."

"Just... I want to see something."

She ducked inside, then reappeared. Something small flew out of the window and hit his shoulder. It was a keychain. He bounced the thing on the palm of his hand. On the keychain, he saw darkness. Fangs. It was from the teen vampire series *Twilight*.

Only, it wasn't a *Twilight* keychain at all, he realized. It was from the HBO TV series *True Blood*.

"You ran into the wrong girl if you're expecting to pull one over on me," she said. "I know all about vampires. You're not going to glamour me."

Reginald looked at the keychain for a moment, then tossed it onto the lower step with the buttons. He sighed, then looked at the streetlamp. It was wrought iron. Pretty, for something so utilitarian.

"How old are you?" he asked the girl.

"Ten."

"And your mother lets you watch *True Blood?*"

"She doesn't know what I do," said the girl. "She's not home most of the time."

"Is she home now?"

"Nope. Not for another hour. That's when her second job ends."

"So you walk home by yourself because the church closes at ten?"

"Yep," said the girl.

"I wouldn't let you do that if I was your father," said Reginald. "Or if I was someone who worked at the church."

"It's not far," she said in a voice that suggested the matter was closed. Then she said, "You look pretty bad, Reginald."

"Thanks."

"I mean you look sick. There's something wrong with you."

"I'm very hungry," he said. "I'm not sure what happens to a vampire when they can't feed, but I'm about to find out, and so far it's not so great."

Reginald let his head sag, wondering how long it would be until the sun rose. At least eight full hours, he realized.

He felt more tired than tired. This was too much. He wished his short vampire life could just end now, before he had to endure more torture. What good was it being a hunter who couldn't catch prey? What good was it being a creature of the night who couldn't move with stealth, who couldn't lift a car, who couldn't seduce women into nights of exaggerated, over-the-top sex? He'd given up daytime and donuts to become a vampire. And for what? There was no upside. He'd been a fat outcast in the human world, and he was now a fat outcast in the vampire world. You had to know when enough was enough. You had to have the awareness to quit when you'd hit a dead end.

Behind him, the door opened and closed. He turned, expecting to see that the girl had come out for some reason, but instead he found a steak sitting in a shallow Styrofoam tray and wrapped with cellophane, the way the supermarkets sold them.

A minute later, the girl was back at the window. She looked at the steak, still studiously avoiding Reginald's eyes.

"I don't know if that will help," she said, "but I don't really want you out there when my mom comes home." Then, realizing she may have said something she shouldn't, she added, "Just so you know, she's a runner. I wouldn't waste your energy trying to chase her."

Reginald looked up. "What am I supposed to do? Sink my fangs into it?"

"I don't know. There's blood in there, is all I know, and even though I don't want you to die, I'm sure not going to let you bite me."

Reginald tilted the tray and watched a shallow pool of beef blood roll around at the bottom. It was cow blood, but maybe it would be better than nothing. He was so, so hungry. Tossing his pride aside, he ripped the cellophane off the package and tipped the corner of the tray into his mouth.

He had no experience drinking blood so there was nothing to compare it to, but to Reginald, who was starving, the effect of those few drops of cow's blood was immediate. Warmth rushed through his veins, to his brain, to the tips of his fingers, wrapped his heart in a blanket and gave it a kiss. Then the wave subsided and he simply felt a little less drained, a little less on the edge of death. It was a start.

He bit the steak with his fangs and tried to suck the blood out of it. It didn't have working arteries, so no gush of blood came out, but he found he was able to suck the liquid out of the spongy tissue. He squeezed it. He licked it like a lollipop. He even tried to wring it out into his mouth. And then, after he'd gotten out all of the blood that was forthcoming and had licked his fingers, he ate it piece by piece. Slowly it went down, and as it did, there was a quenching noise in his stomach. Then he realized he felt *alive* — or at least, as healthy and alive as he'd felt a week ago, as a human.

Reginald took a deep breath of relief and blew it out between pursed lips. "Thank you, Claire," he said. "That was fantastic. I don't know how to thank you." He thought that human courtesy was probably beneath vampires, but he was still mentally more human than vampire and the girl had just saved his life.

"You can go home now," she said. "Before my mom gets back."

"That's a good idea," said Reginald. "I didn't get any sleep last night." But that wasn't right. "I mean, last day," he amended.

He stood up, gave Claire a small wave, and walked down the stairs. He'd turned onto the sidewalk when the girl called to him again.

"Hey, Reginald," she said.

He turned.

"Will you come back and visit?" she said.

"Yeah?"

"Yeah. Mom's got extra hours all this week. Every day, into the night. It gets boring here." Then she raised a hand at him, palm out. "Just so you understand, this isn't an invitation inside my house. You are *not* invited inside. I'm just saying, you know... come back. We've got steaks in the freezer. I'll thaw some for you."

Reginald nodded. "Sure. It's a date."

# TOO FAT

MAURICE RETURNED THE NEXT NIGHT, on Sunday. He asked Reginald how things had gone while he was away. So to punish Maurice for leaving him alone, Reginald told him *exactly* how things had gone. He told him about the three failed attempts at feeding, and then he told him about the steak and how he'd graciously accepted it, going so far as to bring the styrofoam tray home so that he could repeatedly lick it clean.

Maurice made a face.

"What else could I have done?" Reginald asked. "I'm a fat guy who can't eat. I was desperate."

"Well," said Maurice, "you could have fed on the pizza man that first night. That was kind of what I meant for you to do."

"I told you, I wasn't hungry enough yet," said Reginald. "I didn't get hungry until a few nights later. After you'd abandoned me."

Maurice didn't take the bait.

"You *can* feed on animal blood, and you can feed on dead blood, like you did with the steak," said Maurice. "Both are terribly poor substitutes, and combined like that — *dead* blood that is also *cow* blood, and filled with food coloring at that — is the equivalent of being a human and digging through a trash can to find uneaten parts of hamburgers that have been sitting in the sun for two days. If you can keep it down, it'll keep you alive, but... *ugh*."

"It tasted good," said Reginald.

"You probably have a forgiving palate anyway, and when you're that hungry, anything will taste good," said Maurice. "But it's like I said — *not feeding won't kill you*. It just makes you very weak, and it can be quite painful. As you know."

"Well," said Reginald, an edge of resentment in his voice, "thanks for leaving me to mere torture instead of death."

Maurice, his good humor maddeningly intact, sat forward and patted Reginald on the legs.

"Okay," he said. "Let's talk about that. Did I tell you why I was called away?"

"You said it had something to do with the Vampire Nation. That's all."

"Ah. Well, yes. The Nation as a whole, but more specifically the Vampire Council, which is our local ruling body. We've never gotten along, the Council and I, because our society used to be hierarchical based on age, and I'm older than everyone on the council, including its leader. Under the old system, that would make me superior to all of them. Now, I don't have a taste for politics, but the current leader of the council — a man named Logan — has *such* a taste for politics that he can't help projecting his lust onto everyone else. To him, those like me — and there are a handful of us, and plenty who are younger but still old enough to remember how it was before the current regime — have always been a threat. But because I've always just 'had a lot of old-fashioned ideas' and have never directly challenged them, the whole thing has just kind of simmered. We don't like them and they don't like us, but we just kind of let each other be. But then, a few weeks ago, I did something big enough that they couldn't ignore it... and when Charles and Isaac brought me a sort of summons, I killed Isaac. It had nothing to do with his duties as errand boy, and he and his girlfriends were definitely out of line, but vampire/vampire killings are frowned upon. So that was strike two. But strike two got lost in the shuffle immediately, when I committed strike three that same night."

"And that was?" said Reginald. He wanted to stay pissed off himself, but it was hard not to be intrigued by Maurice's recounting of vampire politics.

Maurice held out his hand, palm up, at Reginald.

"Me?"

"You remember how I told you that people train before they become vampires?" said Maurice. "That's a relatively new thing. We used to procreate naturally, turning people as we saw fit, often to create eternal friends and companions. But that meant a lot of 'imperfect' vampires — people like you and me, who have our flaws — and progress always seems to want to march on, to trend toward 'bigger and better and faster.'

"Vampire culture is very animalistic. Just for an example, the classic way to ascend to the head of the Nation is to assassinate the current head of the Nation. It's been buried in bureaucracy and we have a farce of democracy nowadays, but that core is still there, and still very true. The strongest among us tend to survive, and so a few hundred years ago, our whole society underwent a change designed to help us survive in a world where humans were increasingly powerful and self-aware. It made sense at the time to a lot of vampires. It *did* make us stronger and faster and more elusive, but it also created a race to the top. Each generation of vampires since has tried to be a little stronger, a little faster. The bar just keeps getting higher and higher."

"Sounds like the Olympics," said Reginald.

"Exactly. But it all happened slowly, and at the time, it all made sense. Why *shouldn't* the Nation keep track of new vampires? Nobody saw the harm. Then they created a system of orientation, to teach new vampires the things they needed to know, so that they'd be able to function and wouldn't give all of us away. That made sense, too. Then orientation became a class that people could take *before* becoming vampires, to help inform the decision they were about to make. That was sensible. Then orientation became bootcamp, complete with physical training. Then that training became more or less mandatory. Today, there's a whole system — with controls, regulations, even applications — in place for people who want to become vampires. It's no less bureaucratic than the bureau of motor vehicles."

"So it never 'just happens' anymore?" said Reginald. "You have to... what... get permission? Because I've got to say, that sounds really funny coming from a race of cold-blooded killers."

"Procreation accidents like ours do happen," said Maurice. "It's frowned upon, and it's very much fringe behavior — on par with humans who undergo extreme body modification. Usually the creator vampire isn't punished, but the new progeny is almost always treated like a baby with a terrible birth defect for his or her entire life, and the creator is usually shunned for willfully subjecting another to a flawed eternity. But it does happen, and when it does, it usually just means a few more forms and a bit more hassle, like if you forgot to renew your license plates until months after they'd expired. But you..."

"Me?" said Reginald.

"Well, let's just say that you're a bit farther outside of what our society is used to even in the most spontaneous of accidents. *Quite* a bit farther."

Maybe it was his new vampire nature or the fact that he'd starved himself into exhaustion in Maurice's absence, or simply the fact that he was tired of taking shit from everyone — human *and* vampire — but Reginald found himself getting angry again.

"Just say it, Maurice," he said. "I'm like trying to get license plates renewed after the car in question drove off a cliff, exploded, dissolved into ash, and then gained three hundred pounds."

Maurice sighed. "Frankly, yes."

"So... what? Why did they call you in? I'm assuming it wasn't just to yell at you."

"They want to evaluate you," said Maurice. "If they like what they see, you'll go through the normal registration processes, retroactively, and life will go on. If they don't, you'll be destroyed."

Well. That was blunt.

"Can I impress them with my speedreading?" Reginald asked.

Maurice shook his head. "I doubt it. The evaluation is a standard thing. I could show you videos; it's all public record. It's composed of physical tests. No real weight is given to the mental."

"Can I pass it?"

"I don't see how."

"So the evaluation is a formality," said Reginald. "You're basically telling me I've been sentenced to death."

"That may be a little fatalistic, but it's probable."

"Then I'll run. In a car, I mean."

"You can't run," said Maurice, shaking his head. "Nobody really knows where our authorities watch, but we know it's all very Big Brother and that they don't miss much. I might try it if it were just me, but you don't exactly blend in."

Reginald threw up his hands. "Am I just supposed to stay here and wait to be killed? Between no chance and a tiny chance, I'll take the tiny chance. What do I have to lose?"

"Well, one thing I didn't tell you is that the Council plays dirty," said Maurice. "People have run in the past, so the Council has found a solution to that particular problem. They simply start killing everyone the runner knows until they return or until they run out of people and vampires to kill. So your mother and father, any siblings, childhood friends, you name it..."

"Do you think they'd kill Todd Walker?"

Maurice grinned. "Definitely."

"Then I'm definitely running," said Reginald.

Maurice chuckled.

Reginald sat down, then sighed.

"Okay. Fine. I won't run. So what now?"

"We'll go to the Council. A week from Wednesday."

"Where is it?"

"Nobody knows. It moves. Part of Logan's paranoid regime. Someone will come for us, and we'll go with them."

"And in the meantime?"

Maurice stood up and brushed at his pantlegs. "The best way to make a good impression while you're waiting is to demonstrate your ability to follow directions and blend in," he said.

"And what does that mean?" said Reginald.

Maurice went to the door, opened it, and tipped Reginald a goodbye salute. "Tomorrow is Monday," he said. "I'd suggest you go to work."

# NIGHT SHIFT

THE FOLLOWING EVENING AT TEN o'clock, Reginald arrived for his first night on the night shift, made a pot of coffee, and walked back to his cubicle feeling strangely content.

On his way to work, he had stopped by the church he'd visited on Saturday night and waited for the kids to come out into the play yard. Once they did, he found Claire and called her over to a corner. She came toward him easily, and he found himself wondering if, once she got close enough, he could grab her and bite her. But when she got within ten feet, she all of a sudden jumped as if goosed, then turned and ran in the other direction. Reginald was about to leave, dispirited, when she ran back out, hiding something under her coat. When she got close, she pulled out what looked like an enormous brain. It turned out to be a five-pound bulk tray of ground beef, on a white Styrofoam tray, wrapped in cellophane.

"They had it in the cafeteria fridge," she explained.

Though she still wasn't meeting his eyes, she *was* close enough to grab... but he looked down at the beef and felt his insides soften as if she'd given him a teddy bear. Maurice's reservations aside,

Reginald still didn't have anything to compare dead beef blood to, and he couldn't help but be touched.

"Thanks," he said.

He told Claire that he couldn't come over to visit. He said he had to go to work and apologized. She seemed disappointed — said she'd even thawed him a few steaks — but then something bright leapt into her eyes and she asked if he got off work when it was still dark. He said that his shift ended at seven and that as it stood, he'd have to very carefully make it home while the sun was shining — a notion that fascinated Claire, who didn't see how that was possible. Her face fell again, but she said she understood.

Then, as Reginald was turning to leave, again thanking Claire for the pile of ground beef that he was already starting to pick at, he said that he could probably visit on his lunch break, if that wasn't too absurd. She said that it wasn't absurd in the least, and so they arranged to meet at a ground floor window on the side bordering an empty house and away from her mother's bedroom. She promised to leave him a chair so he wouldn't have to stand or sit on the grass.

Then he went to work, wondering if it was odd that his two best friends were turning out to be an impossibly old vampire who looked eighteen and a ten-year-old girl. If anyone was watching him, they'd think he was a pedophile. But that was the good thing about being a social misfit — it didn't matter too much what other people thought, because they were constantly thinking the worst anyway.

With his coffee in hand, Reginald walked into his cubicle and sat down on his cushion. A loud farting noise came from beneath him.

Reginald closed his eyes and asked both God and whoever oversaw vampires for his money back.

A head with perfect teeth and a perfect cleft chin popped over the cubicle divider like a jack in the box. A hand stole over the perfect teeth to keep in an outright burst of laughter. What escaped instead were chortles. The eyes squinted to slits and tears brimmed at the corners.

"Hey!" said the perfect head of Todd Walker once it had gotten its laughter under control. "Welcome to the night shift, Reggie!"

"Todd?"

"You and I are like hair in a braid, Reggie. After you said you had to go to the night shift on account of your skin-melting disease, Phil moved me back here too."

And Reginald, in addition to wondering if it was legal for Berger to tell people about his "skin-melting disease," thought: ... *to torture me?*

"You'll be here all night?" said Reginald, fishing the Whoopee Cushion out from under his seat cushion and dropping it in the trash.

"3pm to midnight," he said. "I'm like an ambassador, bridging the worlds of night and day.

I didn't want to do it, but at least I got a big pay raise."

Reginald didn't take that very obvious bit of bait.

"Besides," said Walker, "the night shift isn't all bad." At this, he nodded toward the door, where a tall, dark-haired woman was walking in and hanging up her coat. She looked like she was probably in her late twenties, dressed in a black skirt and black sweater with a white shirt peaking out from underneath. She was wearing heels, but even without them she was tall. Reginald, who was both tall *and* big, noticed that she almost hit her head on the low EXIT sign that he often ran into himself.

The woman walked in their direction, coming between the rows of cubicles. Walker raised his cleft chin and displayed his perfect white teeth.

"Hey Nikki," he said.

"Hey Todd," she said.

"What are you doing after work?"

"Sleeping."

"Want any company?"

She rolled her eyes humorlessly and walked past them, into the kitchen.

"IT specialist, like your buddy," said Walker. "Apparently she's also a pianist. Pianist. Pianist. I wonder if she likes all things that sound like 'pianist.'" Big grin. Reginald noticed that Walker was speaking to him about the night shift girl the way he'd talk about marathon running to a person in a wheelchair.

With nobody to talk to except for Reginald, Walker was harder than usual to shake. When Reginald had worked the day shift, Walker had been a pest. Now, he was a friendless pest who, in addition to torturing Reginald, seemed willing to take any conversational port in a storm. And most of what he seemed to want to talk about was how hard he was going to nail Nikki once he broke through her veneer.

With the unexpected and unwelcome addition of Walker, the first part of the night shift went much the same as the day shift always had. Reginald didn't have a window, so large stretches of time passed where nothing seemed different, with Walker raising his petty annoyances every few minutes. The only real difference was that when he went into the kitchen for coffee (which he still very much enjoyed, just like pizza, fried chicken, and the rest), he ran into Maurice, with whom he exchanged a few words. He also ran into the new girl, except that she wasn't exactly new. Maurice said she'd been working at the company for as long as he had.

Walker left at midnight and the world became blessedly quiet. It was as if a weight had been lifted off of Reginald, but he wasn't the only one who felt the change.

"Oh, hey, did it just get less assholish in here?" the not-new new girl said aloud as she watched the door close behind Walker.

Reginald looked up. It seemed unlikely she was precisely talking *to him*, but he was the only other person within earshot. So he smirked, but said nothing.

"Now the party can start, right?" she said. This time she definitely *was* talking to him.

Reginald smiled, then looked down.

"Reginald, right? I'm Nikki. I would have introduced myself earlier, but I've been socially beaten down since that jerk started working nights. It's like living under a totalitarian regime." She extended a hand.

Reginald decided that this was the largest number of words a woman had voluntarily said to him in ten years. Reginald shook her hand. It was small but strong, and soft as powder.

"Have you met Maurice?" she said, gesturing. "He wears a sword on his belt."

"Yeah, we knew each other from before. We overlapped a bit when I worked days."

She nodded. "Well, nice to meet you." And she turned to go.

Being the only three people in the office, Nikki, Maurice, and Reginald pinged past each other for the rest of the night like the last few bingo balls left in the hopper.

"How's your hunger?" said Maurice, who he ran into a bit later. "Did you feed yet?"

"Um... kind of," said Reginald.

Maurice made a face.

"I'm going out for lunch," Reginald added.

At 2am, Reginald put on his coat, nodded to Maurice, and headed out to his car. He drove the few miles to Claire's house and, suddenly very aware of how bad all of this could look, parked a block away and approached on foot via a small alley behind the row of houses. As he walked, he decided that this was a dumb idea. Not only was he fraternizing with a little girl through her window in the middle of the night, but she probably wouldn't even be awake. Kids said dumb things, then forgot them.

But as he rounded the corner between Claire's house and the abandoned house next door, he saw a chair sitting on the grass next to a window. A light was on in the window, and as he approached, the sash raised and a small head wearing an anorak hood stuck out and smiled.

"Reginald!" she said.

Reginald shushed her, then scampered up to the window. "Your mom will hear you!" he said. "And for the same reason, are you sure you want that light on?"

"She's totally passed out drunk," said Claire. "I could set the house on fire and she wouldn't flinch."

"Oh."

Claire read his facial expression. "It's okay. She does it all the time."

"Oh."

"I mean, I'm used to it."

"Gotcha."

Claire sighed inside of the giant fur hood. "I shouldn't've said anything. Now you're going to think she's a sleazy drunk. She's not. She's really nice. But it's been hard on her, raising me alone, and she has to work two jobs and I think it just sometimes gets her."

"It's just the two of you?"

Claire nodded.

"Do you ever do anything together? Like, hang out?" Reginald, whose own mother was perhaps too attentive, admitted to himself that he might not have an objective frame of reference, but it seemed like all Claire's mom did was to work and sleep. Without any father, siblings, or other family, he could imagine Claire spending hour after hour after hour alone in the ramshackle house. Watching *True Blood*.

"We had a party for my birthday," she said. "And we always eat dinner together if she's home."

This was too depressing. He opted to change the subject.

"When do you sleep?" he asked her, gesturing at the encompassing night with his eyes. Then he smirked at her. "Are you a vampire?"

"I got up just for you, Reginald. I'd normally sleep now, like a normal girl."

"C'mon. Let me see your fangs."

"I don't have fangs." She giggled like a little girl, because she was one despite her resilient exterior. It was perhaps the first sheen of youth he'd seen from her, he realized. The thought made him sad.

"I'd like to, though," she said.

Reginald shook his head, not understanding.

"I'd like to be a vampire. Tell me... how does it happen? How do you get turned?"

"You wouldn't want to be a vampire," he said, thinking of how everywhere you went, a group in power was telling you that you weren't good enough. At least humans had daytime to spread their intolerance around in.

"I would, though," she said. "I'd be a good hunter. How is it done, Reginald?"

He shook his head and shrugged. "I don't know." And he told her the story of how he'd been turned, exactly a week ago now.

"And now Maurice, my friend... my 'maker,' I guess is the word you'd know... he's in trouble for turning me. And I'm... well..."

"You're what?"

He sighed. "I'm a fat vampire."

"So what?"

"I'm slow. I'm weak. I didn't know in advance, and didn't prepare." Then, because he knew the sorts of things she'd say if he paused there, added playfully, "What about you, Claire? Have you done your training? Have you been hitting the weights? Make a muscle. Show me."

She curled her biceps into an invisible peak. Reginald made impressed noises.

After a few minutes of silence, she looked him in the eyes. Reginald realized he could easily glamour her, but he no longer wanted to.

"I'd like you to turn me," she said. "Not now, obviously. You'll need to figure out how it's done for sure, but then I want in."

"You want *in*?"

"I spend all day in a stupid school that I hate and then I come home and spend nights either literally alone or pretty much alone here, watching TV. This neighborhood isn't great. Sometimes there are shots outside at night. I'm little for my age. I get picked on."

Reginald thought of how easily she'd bested him on the night they'd met, how she'd spun out of his grip as if his hands had been greased. He thought she must do okay, but Reginald knew what it was to be picked on — how it dug into your spirit like talons — and said nothing.

"If I were a vampire," she said, "I'd be on top. I wouldn't just hang out here alone. I could go out at night. I wouldn't have to be afraid of anything."

Then she looked right at him, waiting.

"You're serious."

"Yes. Can you find out how it's done?"

"I can't do that, Claire. Even if I wanted to." And he explained about the training, about the reason that the only vampires anyone ever heard of were fit and thin and strong and fast and attractive. "Besides, he said, you'd never grow up. It's bad enough to know I can never lose weight, but to know you'd be a kid forever? It gets better as you grow up, Claire. Not always a lot better, but for now, you just have to put in your time."

She'd been staring past him, to the side, toward the front sidewalk. Her face didn't move when he was done speaking, but a single tear began to fall down the side of her nose and nest in the hollow above her upper lip.

"Then can you come inside for a while and just sit with me? Just watch TV with me for a while?"

"Are you inviting me inside your house?" he asked.

"Yeah."

He nodded solemnly, picked up the chair and moved it to the back porch, and entered the back door as Claire held it for him.

She made microwave popcorn and they sat on the threadbare couch together watching whatever came on, which just so happened to be the last half of an episode of *Columbo*. There was no stirring from elsewhere in the house, and Reginald thought how disturbing it was that a girl could invite a stranger into the living room and the only authority in the house would never know.

Claire curled up and put her head in his lap, and within ten minutes of finishing her popcorn, she was asleep. He slipped out from under her, replacing his lap with a pillow, and covered her with an afghan.

As he left, being careful not to make any noise, he looked back at the little girl who wanted to be a vampire so that she could be as strong as she tried to feel, the little girl that he couldn't bring himself to feed on.

She looked very small.

# RUT

THE SECOND HALF OF REGINALD'S shift was far better than the first half, now that Walker was gone and his only co-workers were Maurice, who he already knew and liked, and Nikki, who seemed to loathe Walker as much as he did.

Over the rest of the time before his assessment by the Vampire Council, Reginald found himself falling into a nice rhythm. He'd wake as the sun was setting, eat a breakfast of human food out of habit, shower, get dressed, and head off to work. The church where he'd met Claire was on the way, so he always stopped for five minutes to say hello. Then he went to work and he, Maurice, and Nikki endured Walker until he'd gone.

After midnight, a new mood descended over the office. It was still work, but because there were only three of them working and all three got along, the place had a slumber party feel. Without Walker's distractions, Reginald found himself able to complete his work well before his shift was over — and without Berger there to tell him to do more, he simply ended up with free time. Some nights, he played wastebasket basketball with Maurice and Nikki, who seemed to have discovered the same efficiency long ago and had been waiting for Reginald to catch up.

Each night at 2am, Reginald took his lunch break and went to visit Claire. He tried to talk her out of it, saying she needed her sleep and that her mother was bound to, at some point, come downstairs to find her daughter hanging out with a three hundred and fifty pound stranger who she could easily catch if she decided to pursue as he fled — and having promised that he'd feed on neither Claire nor her mother, *flee* he would. But Claire was having none of it. She promised him steaks and hamburger as enticement and said that besides, Reginald's visits were the highlights of her day because he was one of the only friends she had. The notion was depressing beyond belief to Reginald.

He returned to the office around three. His shift was supposed to last until seven, but Nikki, who confessed she knew about the odd disease that her two co-workers coincidentally shared, offered to cover for both from six until she left at eight. So Reginald would go home while it was still dark, draw his blinds, and sit inside watching TV for a few hours, and eventually he'd fall asleep.

One day, when Reginald returned from lunch, he sat down in his seat and heard a loud farting noise. He looked between his legs and saw the pink lips of a Whoopee Cushion.

There was a low chortling, and then a head popped up from Walker's cubicle, saying, "What, Reggie, did someone step on a duck?"

It was Nikki. She was holding Walker's coffee cup, sticking her teeth out in imitation of his giant white tombstones, and letting her lower jaw hang slack. Oddly, the Walker parody did nothing to diminish her beauty.

Reginald laughed, hard. It was the first time he'd laughed — genuinely *laughed*, with all of his mind and body — in as long as he could remember.

Nikki put down the coffee cup and rested her arms across the cubicle divider.

"What are you doing after work, Reggie?" she said, still imitating Walker's voice. Then, in her own voice: "I know a 24-hour piano bar. Maurice and I are getting out of here and going over at five. They're a bit dodgy, but it's the only piano bar in this part of town that's open at five AM and serves waffles, so our choice is limited."

Reginald loved waffles.

"Count me in," he said.

# HOT CHICK

WHEN THEY ARRIVED AT THE piano bar, the official pianists were long asleep or drunk, so the manager, who Nikki knew (probably through the bonds that form amongst pianists) said it'd be fine if they tinkered with the piano on and off while eating their waffles — or, in Maurice's case, while he was drinking his coffee.

Nikki was in her element. Upon receiving the go-ahead and before her waffles arrived, she sat down on the bench, opened one of several sheet music books from a rack beside the piano, and began to play. It was beautiful. It made *her* more beautiful. As she played, she sat taller, and Reginald could swear that something inside of her began to glow in the way he'd seen his own human blood glow that first night on the hill.

While she was playing, Maurice leaned over and said to Reginald, "Have you thought of feeding on her?"

A counterpointing thought crossed Reginald's mind, and he was surprised to realize how deeply it bothered him. Rather than answering the question, he asked Maurice what had occurred to him. "Have *you* fed on her?" he said.

Maurice chuckled. "The only woman I feed on is my wife."

"You have a wife?"

"Yes. And one thing you'll learn is that in the vampire world, we have as many strange, nonsensical conventions as humans have. One is that if you're pledged to another, it's considered infidelity to feed on a human of the same sex as your spouse."

"Your wife is a human?" Reginald said.

"No. She's vampire. But both of us have to feed, and so she feeds on women and I feed on men. Mostly goth kids, who are totally into it."

"That doesn't make any sense at all," said Reginald. "That would be like saying that if I were married, I couldn't eat nachos. I could only eat cheeseburgers."

"It's probably because the act of feeding is, for us, very close to sex when we're feeding on someone we're attracted to. The lines blur. My wife and I feed on each other while... well, you get the idea. But drinking another vampire's blood doesn't nourish us, so we have to eat somewhere. This is how our society has chosen to answer that particular sticky problem. For humans, the lines don't blur. You're not almost having sex with nachos when you eat them."

Reginald thought that Maurice had never seen him eat nachos.

"So," Maurice said. "*Have* you thought of feeding on her?" He nodded at Nikki.

"Very much."

"So glamour her, then feed."

"I can't," said Reginald. "I thought of it when you went to the bathroom. She was looking right into my eyes, but I couldn't do it."

Maurice smiled. "Why?"

"It felt wrong."

"So you've given up feeding on her, then?"

But Nikki interrupted the conversation by returning. She looked flushed and deeply pleased. Something radiated off of her and again, Reginald found himself looking longingly at her neck as her hair moved. He fought it down.

"Shit," said Nikki, looking at the new arrival on the plate in front of her. "How long was I playing? My waffle is cold."

"You know," said Maurice, "Reginald plays piano."

Reginald shook his head. "No I don't."

"Yes you do."

"No I don't," Reginald repeated.

Maurice turned to Nikki. "Hey, could you do me a favor? I need a tissue, but there was no toilet paper in the men's room and I don't feel like blowing my nose on these cloth napkins. Could you grab me a handful from the ladies'?"

She nodded, got up, and walked toward the bathroom. Reginald watched her go.

Maurice slid something into Reginald's hand. It was his phone, and the website on the screen was HowToPlayPiano.com.

"Read it," said Maurice.

"I can't learn to play piano from reading a page on a website," said Reginald.

"You already know how to play the music, believe me," said Maurice. "You just need to know what the notes mean and which keys to hit."

"I have no idea how to play piano," said Reginald. "Seriously."

"Read it. Hurry, before she gets back."

So, because Maurice hadn't been wrong yet, Reginald quickly read the single long page on the screen. He gave the phone back as Nikki was coming out of the bathroom. She handed a wad of toilet paper to Maurice, who thanked her, and again begin slaying her waffle.

"So as I said," Maurice repeated, "Reginald plays piano beautifully." And after much nudging and pushing and cajoling, Reginald found himself sitting on the bench in front of the piano, a dozen or so bleary-eyed patrons staring up at him. The bench groaned under his weight. He couldn't get close enough to the piano until he forced it, folding his gut under the keyboard, and even then he felt stretched out. The book of music Nikki had been playing from was still on the piano. He picked it up and began to flip the pages, totally unsure of what would be good to start with. Something easy.

He looked at Maurice, who nodded encouragement.

The book was filled with different pieces, none of which were remotely familiar to him. Finally he found one by Beethoven, who was at least a name he recognized. The piece was called *Hammerklavier*, and because Reginald had a little bit of German, he knew that "klavier" meant "piano." It seemed as good a starting point as any.

He placed his fingers on the keys and tried to let his mind go back to the place he'd found last week, when Maurice quizzed about passages in *The Shining*. He didn't know how to play. He didn't know how to play. Then, from somewhere in a fog, he kind of did. He knew a few of the first notes on the page in front of him. He could see how they fit together, like pieces in a jigsaw puzzle.

He played the notes.

Then he saw how the next few fit, and played those.

As he fell into rhythm, his fingers seemed to figure out what to do. They knew whether to strike the keys hard or to touch them gently. He stopped seeing the notes on the page and simply saw the music in his mind. The page was irrelevant. He knew what the music was supposed to be. He could see it as if he were solving a problem. One note led logically to the next, to the next. He closed his eyes. The room disappeared. He played by feel, both in his fingers and in his mind. He saw the piece as a whole, even though the whole hadn't been in the book. But it was too long. He finished a section and spun off, into something new. Something from inside himself. And he played. And he *did* know how to play.

Some time later — though he had no idea how long — his fingers pecked out a few final notes and he realized, quite suddenly, that he was done. And so he stood up, returned to the table, and resumed eating.

Across from him, Nikki looked like she'd been slapped. There was a tear running down her cheek.

# SOUL

NIKKI HAD ALWAYS BEEN POLITE and friendly, but in the days that followed, she seemed much more interested in Reginald than could be explained by politeness or friendliness alone.

There was much more smiling and small talk in the halls. They had coffee together in the kitchen, where Nikki kept prodding Reginald about how he had learned to play piano so well. They even hung out twice more at the piano bar — both times alone, because Maurice declined.

Then one day, Nikki asked Reginald to go with her to Taco Bell, which was one of the only restaurants open at 2am. Reginald, who loved Taco Bell, said that he would *really* like to go, but that he was meeting someone. This was intriguing to Nikki, and she asked who could possibly want to meet with him at two in the morning.

At this point Reginald tried to change his story, but he was a bad liar and Nikki was both persistent and beguiling. And so finally, he told Nikki that he had a standing appointment with his 10-year-old niece. He thought that Nikki would find it very odd that Reginald would visit his niece in the middle of the night, but once he told her that his niece had the same sun-wasting disease that he had, she nodded knowingly and said, "I gotcha," and seemed to accept it. Then she asked to come along.

Reginald tried to refuse, but Nikki was both persistent and beguiling.

So Nikki went along, and this time all three of them sat in Claire's living room, watching *Columbo* and eating popcorn, while her mother laid upstairs in a drunken slumber.

Nikki fell absolutely in love with Claire, who she said reminded her of herself as a girl. She told Claire that she wished *she* had her as a niece, and Claire, to whom Reginald had covertly whispered the lie to which she should adhere for the evening, nodded eagerly. She said she'd *love* to have Nikki as an aunt and Reginald as an uncle and then smiled knowingly, and then all three of them chuckled until Reginald caught Nikki's eye and suddenly became terribly embarrassed.

Nikki and Claire enjoyed each other so much (devolving into actual, literal hair-braiding and nail-painting at one point) that Reginald and Nikki didn't arrive back at the office until after four. Reginald apologized to Maurice, who he found shooting staples into a trash can, and Maurice said that he was getting really good at shooting staples and hadn't realized they were gone.

The next evening — the final evening before Reginald's appointment with the Vampire Council — Nikki and Reginald went out to dinner before work. The lighting was low. There were candles on the table. It was almost like a date, except that she was a hot girl and he was fat Reginald. Otherwise, the resemblance between their dinner meeting and a date was uncanny. Reginald even made an effort to dress up, in the spirit of what felt like an occasion. Nikki wore a dress with a slit up the side. She promised to change into something more boring before going to work lest she blow Walker's mind, or lest she find herself fending off his grabby hands until midnight.

"You don't think he'd actually grab you, do you?" said Reginald.

"Yeah, I do," she said. "And in fact, I kind of hope that one day he does."

Reginald almost took this the wrong way, but then she explained that she'd been practicing Krav Maga since her father had started making her attend lessons at age six, when it had become apparent that she'd be pretty.

"That fucking guy," said Reginald. Then, demurely, he put a hand in front of his mouth, as if he'd shocked himself. He didn't swear much, and certainly not in front of women. Swearing, in Reginald's mind, implied confidence, which he'd never had much use for.

"It's okay," said Nikki. "He definitely is 'that fucking guy.'"

"Asshole," said Reginald.

"Motherfucker," said Nikki. Then she giggled, a sound that for some reason made Reginald's blood hunger rise to the back of his throat. She brushed a loose hair off of her neck. Her neck was long and white, and Reginald had to suppress an almost irresistible urge to leap over the table and sink his fangs into it.

"I'd like to be forward, Reginald," she said. "May I?"

"Sure."

"You're better than you think you are."

Reginald didn't know what to say to that. It *was* forward. For one, it was presumptuous to tell him who he was. For two, it implied that he didn't think much of himself. And for three, he didn't care and hearing her say it made him feel good.

"Thanks."

"I mean it, Reginald. I see how Walker is with you, and I see how you avert your eyes when people talk to you. Can I be even more forward?" Then she answered herself, laughing: "Why stop now? Okay, I'll say it. Just because you're big doesn't make you less than that asswipe, or any of those other asswipes. Our society is messed up. We judge people by how they look. But you? You're better than the Walkers of the world. The soul you showed when you played the other night? It's beautiful."

"My soul?"

"Yes. Music comes from the soul," she said matter-of-factly.

"I thought that one came from Beethoven," said Reginald.

"Well," she said, "forgetting for a moment that *Hammerklavier* is one of the most difficult pieces

I know of — especially for someone who 'just learned by playing around' — you spun off on your own at the end. Where did that come from?"

"I don't know. I guess my gut." Then, realizing the pun, he patted his gut and laughed. "It does have some authority."

"It came from your soul. Your soul is beautiful."

Reginald thought that her breasts were beautiful. He felt guilty thinking something so shallow, but then he decided it was okay because he liked a lot about her, and her chest was just one part of an overall delightful whole.

"I like being here with you," she said.

"Why?" said Reginald. He realized how it sounded, but it was a knee-jerk reaction. The word was out before he could stop himself.

"I told you why."

"But... I'm fat. And not terribly attractive."

"Beauty is in the eye of the beholder," she said.

A full minute passed. She reached forward and took his hand.

"I'm a vampire," he blurted.

She nodded. "I know."

"You know?"

"Maurice told me."

"Maurice is a vampire too." This verbal diarrhea was idiotic. He'd rat out his mother for a crime she'd never even thought of committing if he kept it up. Maybe *Nikki* was a vampire. Maybe she was glamouring him right now, except that vampires couldn't be glamoured. And by the way, what a load of crap *that* was.

She smiled. "I know he's a vampire. We've known each other for a while. Things come up. He has some stories that don't make any sense without that particular tidbit."

"Are *you* a vampire?"

"No. But I assume your niece is?"

"My niece?"

"Your niece. Claire? I assumed that's the reason you meet with her at 2am."

Reginald shook his head. "She's not my niece. She's a human I tried to feed on because I couldn't catch anyone else. I couldn't catch her either, so she gave me a raw steak. Her mother is always drunk. We get together every night at 2am and watch *Columbo* because she's lonely and doesn't have many day friends."

That was without question the oddest reply that anyone had ever given to anyone, anywhere, ever, but Nikki seemed unfazed by it. She patted his hand, as if 10-year-old, middle-of-the-night playmates were totally normal.

Reginald's head sagged. "I'm a bad vampire. I'm slow. I'm weak. I'm too fat to be undead."

"Maurice says you're smart."

"I guess."

"And he's always told me that vampirism enhances what's in you already," she said. "Which is how I know that your soul is beautiful, with that music you had inside."

Reginald found himself starting to smile, but then his mind floated to tomorrow, to his meeting with the Vampire Council, and the smile left his lips. It seemed unfair that he could have found such contentment so soon before being sentenced to what felt like an inevitable death. He was once a fat kid, then he was a fat adult, and then he'd had two and a half weeks to be a fat vampire. Soon he wouldn't even be that. Soon he'd be ash, and as far as the vampires of the world were concerned, it was good riddance to bad public relations rubbish.

"I'm on trial tomorrow," said Reginald. "Did Maurice tell you that?"

"Yes."

"Do you guys have long conversations while I'm in the bathroom or something?"

"Maurice is my mentor," she said.

"You must not talk about computers much, with all the vampire discussions you have," said Reginald.

"No. I meant, he's my mentor in vampirism," said Nikki.

"He's what?"

She shrugged. "Some people meet a baseball player and decide to become a baseball player. I met a vampire."

"Wait. You're going to become a vampire?"

"Yes. I'm in training. Just finished, actually."

"Ah. Training."

"There's a whole program," she told him. "It's like Six Sigma meets Navy SEALs bootcamp. You'll see."

"I'll see?"

"After your trial. Maurice says you'll have to do it all retroactively. But the good news for you is that they can't decide *not* to turn you since you're already turned, and..."

"Nikki," said Reginald, interrupting her, "I'll never see that training. I've watched some of the 'meetings' from the council records. I know what they'll ask me to do and I can't do it, not even close, and so I'm going to be executed. It's a big puppet show. They just want to humiliate me before they kill me, because I blemish their image."

Reginald didn't tell her the other unsavory things he'd learned from the public records, like how the only way to avoid a quick death in a sun chamber was to commit an additional offense that *really* pissed off the council — in which case you'd be cut open over and over and over before finally being dragged into the sun to die. From what Reginald had seen, the torturers were quite good, and used a wide variety of sharp knives to do their jobs.

Nikki shook her head. "You should run," she said.

At least she wasn't telling him that he might pass his ordeal. That would just be insulting to both of them.

"I can't run," he said, and told her what Maurice had said about what the council did to the families and friends of runners. They'd kill Maurice if they could catch him. They'd kill Nikki.

"We could run, too."

"You can't outrun vampires." That was another thing he'd seen while studying his foes' records. Humans targeted by the Vampire Nation never survived. Never.

"I could turn. I'm ready. Maurice could do it. Or you could."

"I'm going to make it worse by turning you?" He shook his head. "No way. There's no way out. And even if there was, there's all the other people I know. My family. My neighbors and *their* families."

"You could find a way to..."

Reginald interrupted her. "And Claire."

Nikki slowly closed her mouth. Then she said, "Yeah. And Claire."

"But honestly, I'm worried about Claire anyway. The Council is sadistic. The stuff I've watched and read? They don't like to leave loose ends. If anyone knows I've been hanging out with her, which they almost certainly do, I'll find out at the trial. It'll be a nice little surprise before I die. 'Oh, hey, just so you know, we know all about your friend, and we're headed out there now to suck her dry.' They do stuff like that all the time from what I've seen."

"Maurice can protect her."

"Maurice will be with me. Hell, they might just kill him too. He's already said he's on thin ice. That'd be a cool twist, right? Your night shifts might be a lot quieter next week."

Reginald didn't like the way he sounded, but he couldn't help himself. Because the Council's biggest concern was being overthrown by a rising power-seeker, it ruled through fear. The trials Reginald had reviewed were absolutely filled with psychological torture. It made him angry, but there was nothing he could do except to take it out on Nikki, who was the only outlet he had.

"Me, then," she said.

"What *about* you?"

"I'll protect her."

"Nikki..."

"After you turn me, of course."

Reginald raised both of his hands in a warding-off gesture.

"Look," she said, "I'm already cleared. I even got an approval letter. I've got a formal ceremony coming up in a month, but if they do decide to kill Maurice, then it all falls apart because he's my mentor. I'd have to start all over. This is just moving things up a little. And this way, when you and Maurice go in, I can watch the fort here for you."

Reginald tapped a finger on the table.

"Come on, Reginald. Think it through in that big, enhanced brain of yours. What other choice is there?"

He knew the answer, of course: *None.* He'd probably doomed Claire the moment he met her, but he'd almost certainly sealed her fate this week. *Of course* vampires would be watching him in the week before his trial, and of course he'd never have noticed them. Claire couldn't protect herself and she couldn't run. The chances of vampire Nikki protecting her were still incredibly slim, but slim was better than none. Reginald knew how to turn her, too. It was one of many, many things he'd learned over the past few nights about vampirism and vampire culture in his futile search for a way out.

"Are you thinking about it?" she asked him.

"Yes."

"Will you do it?"

He exhaled and began nodding slowly, his big, enhanced brain working through scenario after scenario after scenario.

"Okay," he said. "But I want to do one thing a little differently."

And he told her.

# MORE ASSHOLES

ON THE NIGHT OF THE meeting — which in Reginald's mind had definitely become a "trial" — Maurice came over to Reginald's house and the two sat on Reginald's run-down, bent-in-the-middle couch and watched *America's Funniest Videos* until a knock came at the door.

"Let's not let them in," said Reginald, suddenly nervous.

"This is no longer a human house," said Maurice with a wry smile. "You can't keep them out if they want to come in."

"Oh. Okay."

So he got up, and he walked to the door and opened it. Standing on the stoop under the porch light were Charles, Moira, and Penelope — the three remaining of the foursome he'd met a thousand years ago, back when he was human.

"Hello big boy," said Charles, his eyes full of something Reginald couldn't interpret. "As a duly appointed representative of the Vampire Nation, I, Charles Barkley, bring with me a warrant requiring your presence at..."

"Your name is Charles Barkley?" said Reginald.

Charles ignored him and continued speaking. "... at a meeting of the Vampire Council..."

"Because in your shoes, I'd go by 'Chuck,' or 'Charlie.'"

"... to determine your suitability for inclusion in the population of..."

"Or, you know, just never use your last name."

Charles ceased his delivery and locked eyes with Reginald. "Joke now," he said.

"I'm just saying," said Reginald, who hadn't been joking. He'd once known a man named Ronald Reagan. The man was so liberal, he was left-handed. Reginald had always meant to ask why he didn't just go by 'Ron,' but had never had the nerve.

Charles turned to Maurice. "And *you*. Do you have a death wish? As his maker, you've now committed your third act of treason in a month. Nobody cares how old you are or what rights you seem to think you have, Maurice. You can be staked by the Guard just like anyone else."

"I stand by my creation," said Maurice, with a glance toward Reginald. Then he added, "... and my right to make as I choose."

The women had broken away from Charles and, as they'd done on the night behind the bowling alley, began circling Reginald. Their voices came from behind him, near his ears. Now that he was no longer human, their voices were no longer hypnotic, but they were still a turn on.

"You tasted amazing," said Moira.

"Delirious," said Penelope.

"And now?" said Moira.

"Such a pity," said Penelope.

Reginald whispered to Maurice. "Why did *they* like me so much, yet I made you barf?"

"Why do so many people like McDonald's, yet the grease would make a healthy person keel over?" Maurice answered.

The women came full circle and stood in front of them, one on each side of Charles. All three looked like they could appear in a magazine photoshoot right then, without going to hair, makeup, or wardrobe. Reginald, not even a little bit gay, found even Charles beautiful.

"Quite a pity," Charles agreed, looking Reginald over from head to toe. "A beautiful cut of meat wasted... and a race blemished."

Maurice's hand went to his sword.

"Easy, Maurice. You won't get away with staking me like you did Isaac. I'm on orders from the Guard. You'd burn for it."

Maurice's hand lowered.

"If only you'd come with us when we came for you the first time instead of making your little scene," said Charles with phony regret. "Just think — all of this could've been avoided."

Maurice stared at Charles, his eyes unblinking.

"So," said Charles. "Will you come with us? Or would you like me to leave without you and put your apprehension in the hands of the Guard?"

"I hope they want to tussle first," Moira whispered to Penelope.

Penelope rubbed her breasts. Her fangs snapped out, and she ran her tongue over them. "Me too," she purred.

"We'll come with you," said Maurice.

Penelope's fangs receded and a pout formed on her lips. "Oh, poo," she said.

# TESTED

"WE'RE GOING TO MISS OUR window," said Charles from behind the wheel of the SUV.

Reginald and Maurice were in the rear row of seats, behind Penelope and Moira, behind a silver mesh, restrained by silver handcuffs. Charles wasn't speaking to them, but Reginald knew exactly what he was talking about. In the past week, he'd researched and learned more about the Vampire Council — which shared its protocols openly so that any power-seekers would fully understand the futility of an attack — than he imagined Charles would ever know.

For one, the Council kept its location top secret, even from itself. The entire Council worked like a touring mega-concert, with hundreds of vampire roadies tasked with disassembling, transporting, and reassembling the entire operation every eight, nine, or ten days. The location, specific timing, and coordination of these movements were determined by an incredibly complicated encrypted algorithm. The algorithm was a total black box. The council could request a move, but could not control or predict that move. The only way for Council members to see where the Council would go next was to follow the instructions given by the algorithm and wait until all of the pieces fell into place.

Every eight, nine, or ten days, the algorithm would deliver new sets of orders to the roadies. The algorithm coordinated their travel — via discreet and different paths — to their final location. Dozens of individual surveyors were constantly feeding updated information into the database regarding the suitability of locations, weather and population updates, purchases and sales of real estate, and anything else that might be relevant, and the algorithm drew from all of it. On any given move, the Council might repurpose an abandoned structure, re-use a past location, or build something fresh. The whole production was like a colony of ants obeying orders made by an unseen intelligence.

The only way for anyone to get in or out was to pass through a series of hand-offs involving several pairs of escorts. Because the Council was a moving target, the algorithm coordinated this entire process as well. It was impossible to predict where someone on their way to the Council might be at any given time or what route they might take. Even the escorts didn't know where they were taking their passengers until they were on the road, and theirs was only one leg of a larger route comprising several legs.

Charles was worried because when you were summoned by the Council, the algorithm gave you only a location and a half-hour window of time. If

you missed the window, you missed your chance —
and then, usually, you paid a price.

Charles had three minutes left.

"It would be so much faster to run," said
Charles, "if only I had a secure way to carry that fat
load."

"And me," said Maurice. "Don't forget the fact
that I'd tear your head off the minute we got out."

"You'd never escape," said Charles, taking
another glance at the dashboard clock.

"I didn't say anything about escaping," said
Maurice. "After I killed you, I'd be sure to make
the window. " He would, too. Maurice could argue
that he'd had to kill Charles because Charles was
going to make him late for his pickup. The Council
would accept it as a justified tradeoff.

Charles pulled up to the pickup point, which
turned out to be under a bridge downtown, with
thirty seconds to spare. One of the waiting Guards
was actually looking at his watch as they pulled up
and piled out of the SUV, Maurice and Reginald
held between the others.

"You're almost late," said one of the Guards.

"We call that 'on time' around here," said
Maurice.

The Guard punched Maurice hard in the face.

The other Guard looked at Charles and the
women. "*You're* supposed to come along," he said,
indicating Charles. Then he waved at the women.
"They're not."

The women pouted, purred a goodbye to Reginald, and drove away in the SUV. When they were gone, the Guards put Reginald, Maurice, and Charles into the back of their vehicle, which was also an SUV. There were no windows in the back compartment. All were bound in silver handcuffs and blindfolded twice so that when the doors were opened at subsequent checkpoints, they wouldn't be able to see where they were.

"So where is the Council today?" Maurice asked a Guard as he was preparing to close the door. "I'll bet it's a drive-in. Is it a drive-in?"

There was a thick slugging sound that Reginald assumed was the Guard punching him again.

"Never hurts to ask," said Maurice from somewhere in the darkness once the door had closed. "Well, other than literally."

The SUV drove off, leaving the remains of Reginald's human life behind. He wondered if he'd ever see his house again — and if not, whether his plants would die before someone realized he was missing.

After three transfers to different vehicles, they were offloaded, grabbed by the arms, and told to walk. They proceeded through what seemed to be a long, echo-filled corridor, walked down some stairs, and then traversed another long and winding path somewhere with less echo. There was a flurry of pushing and shoving and clanking, and then Reginald's blindfolds and restraints were removed.

He found himself in a stark, white room with absolutely no decorations or furniture. There were no features on any of the surfaces. The walls were as smooth as glass. The effect was disorienting. If he looked back, right, left, down, or up, he saw the exact same thing. The only feature by which he could orient himself was a set of bars and a cell door, all made of silver.

On the other side of the cell door was Maurice, who was cuffed and bookended by two Guards, but who didn't seem to be bound for a cell.

"This is so futuristic. It's like the ultimate in minimalism," said Reginald.

"Nothing to use against them," said Maurice.

"I'm going to die, aren't I?" said Reginald.

"Probably," said Maurice. "You'll get your chance to defend yourself, but..." He shook his head.

"I've seen the videos on that vampire YouTube. I'm most looking forward to the rock wall, the hurdles, and the rope ladder."

"I'm sorry, Reginald," said Maurice with a shake of his head. "I should have let you die."

Reginald, who had used his short time as a vampire to meet Claire and Nikki, wasn't sure he agreed.

"It's okay," said Reginald. "Thanks for trying. Any advice?"

"Just be yourself," said Maurice. "There's nothing else you can do."

Some time later, Reginald was taken from his cell and led through a door that had previously been invisible on the featureless walls. Two members of the Guard escorted him down a long hall and into a wide open chamber. The floor of the chamber was hard-packed clay. Around the sunken chamber floor were rows and rows of benches filled with spectators. To one side was an ornate wooden chair that looked like a throne, and in the throne sat a man with stark black eyebrows and salt-and-pepper hair. He looked like he might be in his sixties if he were human.

Reginald's escorts uncuffed him and shoved him into the center of the floor, then disappeared. Gaining his footing and looking up, Reginald could see Maurice, seated between two hulking men in Guard uniform.

"My my," said the man in the throne. "You *are* a big boy."

Reginald said nothing.

"Reginald Baskin," said the man. "I am Logan, Deacon of this Council, and it is my duty today to assess you."

Reginald raised a hand. "'Sup."

"You are here to be tried," said Logan. "Do you understand what is expected of you?"

Interesting how it had become a "trial" in everyone's mind, Reginald thought, when it had begun as a "meeting." At least they were all on the same page.

"Not even a little bit," said Reginald. That was a lie, of course, but he wasn't planning to make this easy.

Logan took a deep breath and stood up, then began speaking theatrically, as if reading a script.

"The Vampire Nation requires secrecy and stealth in order to continue to exist," he said. "Because of that, we have, in recent centuries, begun to establish certain standards. Most people, when they wish to become vampires, train for months to achieve the perfectly honed body they will need to be as strong, fast, and lithe as possible, because the body they are turned with will be the body they have forever. It is important that the standards we set for those bodies and skills are high. We have survived for as long as we have because humans refuse to believe we exist, and because we have trained ourselves to be like shadows. The minute we become clumsy and expose ourselves or give humans reason to believe that we are real, the sooner we hasten our own demise. Do you understand?"

Reginald nodded. He wished they'd just get on with it.

"Not all vampires are created equal, Mr. Baskin," said Logan. "And if a vampire is too slow or too weak, he risks exposing all of us. And if such a vampire is a risk, he must be removed from the population."

"Duly noted," said Reginald.

"The purpose of the tests you are about to undergo is to determine if you meet the standards we have set, or if you are a risk to all of us."

"Awesome."

"I hope you won't take this personally. This isn't about you. This is about the very survival of our kind."

"Boom goes the dynamite," said Reginald.

Reginald found himself starting to daydream. In a movie, this would be the point where he'd find strength he didn't know he had, rush the man in the throne, and rip off his head. Then he'd take over Deaconship of the Council and pardon himself, claim a harem, and spend eternity screwing beautiful women.

The only problem, of course, was that Reginald was still too fat and too sluggish to do anything. And even if he'd had the ability to attack anyone, there were no weapons.

"Then let's begin," said Logan, sitting back down.

The tests that followed were a cross between an agility course and something out of *Mad Max Beyond Thunderdome*. While the assembly watched and a man next to Logan took notes, Reginald was asked to run a series of obstacles as fast as possible, to climb under complex metal structures (fail) and leap over others (double fail). The crowd watched as he tried to cross above a pool of water on a rope ladder, but Reginald immediately rolled over so that he was below the

155

ladder, and then fell into the water. Then he got back up and tried again with the same result. Logan insisted he try a third time, and this time he was halfway across and hopeful he could actually make it when the ropes broke and he crashed into a rock near the edge of the pool, breaking his nose.

Reginald failed to lift heavy weights, failed to smash a series of bricks, and failed to catch a ball dropped across the room. (The ball hit the ground, still fifty feet away, as Reginald took his fourth step and then tripped.) He failed to bend bars and climb walls. At one point, a Guard challenged him to the classic "if you can snatch this coin from my hand" cliche from kung fu films, which he failed miserably.

The final straw for Reginald was a jump test, which reminded him of his high school gym class. Back then, the coach used a tall pole with a series of multicolored flags on it that you were supposed to swat aside to determine your best jump height. Logan didn't require such equipment for his version.

"Even the youngest and weakest of us could jump straight up and touch this ceiling," said Logan, pointing up. Reginald looked up and saw a domed ceiling fifty feet above him. "Let's see if you can do it." He made a little wave and added, "If you please."

Reginald crouched, funneled all of his energy into his legs, and leapt. It was actually quite gratifying. He didn't touch the roof, but he'd never jumped so high in his life. Like his vision on that first night, spotting a billboard from a great distance, the feeling was exhilarating.

The man standing beside Logan made a note on a metal clipboard and said, "Approximately nine inches."

"I can do better," said Reginald.

"Go ahead."

This time, Reginald leaped even higher. He put so much into the takeoff, in fact, that when he landed, he canted sideways and fell onto a hurdle from a previous stunt. The hurdle bent neatly in half.

"Nine inches," said Logan's assistant.

Reginald had had enough. He stood up, brushed himself off, and addressed Logan.

"I think that'll do. Clearly I'm not going to pass any of these ridiculous tests, so why don't you just kill me and get it over with? Is it really necessary to keep humiliating me?"

Movement caught the corner of his eye. It was Maurice, slowly nodding. *Yes, it is.*

"Every test you take is one more chance to prove yourself," said Logan. "Are you through trying to prove yourself?"

The jumpsuit Reginald had been given to wear was plastered to his skin with sweat. His heart was beating out of his ribcage. He hadn't had a full chest of breath since the tests had begun.

"Yes," said Reginald.

"You realize that if you give up, your fate will be decided," said the man.

Reginald, who was sure his fate had been decided long ago, said, "I need to sit down." Then he flopped to the ground, panting.

"Are you sure you don't want to wrestle The Thing?" said Logan. A door slid open across the arena. A very large, very muscular, very hairy man was standing in the recess it revealed, dressed in straps of black leather. He seemed to shine, as if he'd been greased.

"Very sure," said Reginald.

The door closed. The Thing looked disappointed.

"Then it's time to pronounce sentence," said Logan.

"Fine," said Reginald, still trying to catch his breath.

"Obviously, you've failed," said Logan.

"Obviously."

"Worse than anyone has ever failed," he added.

"I'm A-Number One."

"Which means you'll need to be killed. Nothing personal, you understand."

Two panting breaths. "Bring it."

"You and your whole bloodline, of course."

"Of course." He stopped. "Wait... what?"

"Bring in his progeny," said Logan.

But that didn't make sense, because Reginald had never had any kids. He'd never been married or even really in a relationship, unless you counted...

*Shit.*

A large door across from him opened to reveal a smaller room off of the main arena. There, in the center, Reginald saw a woman tied to a post with silver chains.

It was Nikki.

# CAUGHT

MAURICE MADE A LOUD NOISE of exasperation when he saw Nikki chained to the post, then put both of his palms to his face. Reginald didn't know if he should watch Maurice or Nikki as the spectacle unfolded, because both appeared to be equally pained.

The side chamber in which Nikki was restrained was maybe fifteen yards across, clay-floored like the arena, and appeared to be round. It was as if there were a silo attached to the main room and that a shared wall had just been removed. Nikki was sitting on the ground at the foot of a metal pole, bound to it by silver chains that allowed her to move in a small circle, like a dog tied to a tree.

She appeared to be crying. Reginald yelled her name, but either she didn't hear him or was too terrified to respond.

"Nicole Jane Pilson," said the man next to Logan, reading off of a piece of paper on what appeared to be a stainless steel clipboard. "Aged twenty-eight human years when turned. Vampire age of one day. Hereby sentenced to death, as tainted blood, in conjunction with the sentencing of Reginald Baskin."

Nikki screamed. The last time Reginald had seen her, she'd looked so confident and strong, and now she seemed weak and broken. Was this how vampires welcomed new members to their ranks? She was only a day old. It was repugnant that the crowd would afford her so little dignity — especially considering she'd completed her training and was going to be turned within a month anyway — simply due to her association with Reginald.

"Nicole Pilson," Logan shouted across the arena, "you are sentenced to die by sunlight exposure as the offspring of Reginald Baskin. Do you understand?"

"No I fucking *do not!*" she yelled. Reginald's vampire sight was good enough to make out every tear on her cheek. She was both angry and terrified, but even under the circumstances, the anger was the dominant of the two. Yes, she would grow to be a formidable vampire — if she were given a chance.

"Reginald!" Nikki yelled. "I tried; I'm sorry!"

Reginald caught her eyes, nodded dejectedly, and said nothing.

"You're not going to tell her that you're the one who's sorry?" said Logan.

Reginald turned his gaze on Logan. He could feel fury building inside of himself like pressure inside of a tea kettle. In his mind, every vampire in the arena was exploding in fire as he found untapped reserves of strength and stormed through the crowd. Heads flew. Blood spattered. Limbs were twisted and torqued until tendons snapped.

Logan shrugged, as if in disbelief at Reginald's lack of chivalry.

Reginald thought: *You dirty motherfucking son of a bitch.*

"Nothing at all?" said Logan. The crowd tittered. "After we've gone to all this trouble to surprise you? That's a shame."

"She's a thousand times the vampire I am," said Reginald. "Test her. You'll see."

"We do these things like pruning a tree. You're where we're cutting the branch. Her abilities don't matter. She's tainted."

"Wasteful," Reginald spat. "Spiteful. Such noble traits for so 'evolved' a race."

Logan chuckled. But then there was movement a bit farther down the bench as Charles rose to his feet.

"Deacon?" said Charles.

Logan looked at the Guards, who had risen to face Charles, and patted the air. Then to Charles: "Yes?"

"I know of another loose end in this man's case," said Charles.

Reginald looked at Charles, who smirked back at him.

"What loose end?" said Logan.

"A girl."

"What girl?" said Logan.

"A human girl. One that Mr. Baskin has made into a pet."

"A pet?"

"He's been going to visit a young girl. Not to feed. Just to sit with her, and talk to her for hours about being a vampire."

Reginald felt that pressure building inside.

*You dirty motherfucking son of a bitch.*

Logan's eyes found Reginald's.

"He hasn't glamoured her. He hasn't fed. He's just... exposed himself?"

"Yes, Deacon."

To Reginald: "The question before this Council was supposed to be whether or not you threaten to expose us accidentally, simply by existing. Have you really been so idiotic as to talk about vampirism openly?"

"She's just a kid. She doesn't have anybody, and I..."

Logan held up his hand. "Reginald Baskin, for both your wanton creation —" He gestured at Nikki. "— and your breach of our secrecy to a human, I hereby change your sentence from death by sunlight to evisceration followed by death by sunlight." Then slapped his throne, probably because he didn't have a gavel.

Charles was still standing. "And the human girl?" he said.

"Dispose of her," said Logan.

Nikki screamed and tugged at her chains. The sound was terrible and desperate and full of

163

sorrow. Reginald could still see Claire in his mind, her small face dwarfed by the large anorak hood. Or asleep on his lap, feeling safe for once in her young life.

"Deacon," said Reginald quietly, penitent. "She's just a kid. She can be made to forget. And even if she spoke, nobody would believe her. Let her live. Please. Let me tell Maurice where she is. Let him be the one to make her forget."

"No need, Deacon," said Charles. "I already know where she is."

"Please," said Reginald. "You have me. It's my fault. Do whatever you need to me, but let the others go."

Logan seemed to be mulling something over in his mind. Then he said to Charles, "Dispose of her."

The Guard with the clipboard made a note.

"Okay," said Logan. "Let's get this over with."

# GUTS

REGINALD COULDN'T BE KILLED TWICE in punishment for his multiple crimes, so to make his ending as unpleasant as possible, Logan explained that he was to be laid down and cut open, over and over, by a torturer. He'd experience the pain of evisceration, which Logan assured him sounded quite unbearable, and then would heal. Once healed, he'd be cut open again, and again, and again. Different torturers put different flavors on the ritual. Some liked to dissect and remove organs. Some liked to repeatedly puncture the lungs and leave the condemned to gasp for breath, unable to go unconscious or die. Some had a neurologist's understanding of physiology and could conjure unworldly pain merely by touching different nerve clusters.

This would go on for hours, until the assembly or Logan got bored. Then Reginald would be dragged into the sun to meet his end, but by then it would really just be about disposal, because he'd almost certainly have gone mad.

While this was going on, as if it wasn't a rich enough experience, he'd also get to watch Nikki die. The round chamber she was in had a roof that would iris open when Logan pushed a button behind his throne, letting in the sun. It was approximately one o'clock in the afternoon, so the sun would be directly overhead — meaning that the crowd, safe in the arena, could remain comfortably in the shadows and watch while she burned.

Reginald was taken to a spot closer to the side chamber and bound with silver chains to a post of his own. He found himself just twenty feet from Nikki — close enough to see every detail of her upcoming ordeal, but far enough away that he wouldn't be able to dive into the sunlight when the roof of the silo was opened. If he did that, it'd spoil all the fun.

He stood face-to-face with Nikki on the hard-packed floor, his eyes staring into hers. Neither said anything, but Reginald's eyes told Nikki that he was sorry, and Nikki's, which had grown strong, told him that it was okay.

A Guard walked to where Reginald stood, put a hand on his chest, and pushed him back so that he was lying in a semi-reclined position with his head propped against a small mound of sand that seemed to have been placed there specifically as a headrest. From his new position, he'd be able to clearly see Nikki as she died while also sufficiently exposing himself to let the torturer do his work.

The Guard unzipped Reginald's jumpsuit to expose his huge white stomach. The air in the arena was very cold.

Up in the bleachers, Logan looked down at Reginald. "Anything to say before we get underway?" he said.

"Yes," said Reginald, from the ground. "I'd like to invite you to go fuck your mother."

Logan smirked.

Two Guards pinned Reginald's hands and legs to the ground. A man wearing a robe and carrying a black leather bag appeared above Reginald, knelt, and then opened the bag. He pulled out an enormous knife, big enough to be called a machete. The edge was so sharp that it seemed to vanish into nothingness.

"This one is predictable," said the man, indicating the giant knife, "but it's a good way to start. We'll have all the time in the world to explore the finer nuances after your girlfriend turns to ash."

Reginald considered spitting in the man's face, but it seemed like too big of a cliche. Besides, Reginald had a policy about unnecessarily angering people wielding knives.

Logan turned to the man next to him and said something. The man pressed something behind the throne.

Standing in front of Reginald, Nikki refused to look up as a rumbling noise began overhead. She looked into Reginald's eyes, her body upright and proud, and silently said goodbye.

The torturer palpated Reginald's gut. He kneaded it like dough. Then he slid the tip of the machete into Reginald. It entered as easily as if it were going into butter. A great torrent of blood lipped up around the blade and spilled to the dirt. The pain was sharp, like the knife, and Reginald felt some part of himself tugged away with the pain. He wanted to scream but refused to let himself, and then the knife was withdrawn and he watched himself heal.

A blinding light spilled down onto Nikki. All of the strength she'd had a moment ago left her and she screamed, holding her hands up and then curling into a ball, trying to shield herself. She began to smoke. Reginald squinted into the light. It hurt his eyes. Looking around the room, he could see that it was hurting the eyes of every vampire in the room, but none of them would look away. Their bloodlust made hateful bile rise in Reginald's throat.

Again the torturer slid the huge knife into his stomach and Reginald's attention was yanked from Nikki and from the crowd. Reginald couldn't help himself this time. He screamed. He thrashed. The Guards held him as firmly as iron girders. Then the knife came out and the wound healed again. He could feel his heart pounding — whether in memory of the pain, anticipation of more, or in fear for Nikki, he didn't know. Then, with barely a pause to let him catch his breath, the blade was back. He felt something pop. The pain this time was beyond the world. His head spun but remained maddeningly conscious and aware, offering no escape into delirium or shock.

The knife went deeper. Wiggled. Hands entered his fat, pulling at guts and organs. Then the hands withdrew and he healed again. The torturer looked down at him without expression, holding up a red, dripping fist.

Reginald squinted into the blinding light in front of him. Nikki had begun to smoke and pop in earnest. There was a sharp sizzle, then a burst of sparks. He yelled her name, but all she could answer with was a fading scream.

The torturer's knife slid back into Reginald. Deeper. He tried to turn away from the pain but couldn't move. It was as if he could actually feel his organs failing, and then, as the knife moved, he could feel them knit and heal. The knife moved back and forth, pausing at each end. He healed after each pass. His skin grew around the blade, and then it would move again. The sensation was maddening.

Nikki's screams were fading. There was more smoke in the air, less from where her body lay motionless. There were sparks. Whimpers.

The knife cut again. Again hands entered his chest, his gut, his huge belly, pushing rolls of fat aside, bloodying the clay and turning it maroon beneath him. The hands pulled and prodded and ripped and tore. And then they stopped.

"What the hell is this?" said the torturer.

Nikki was silent. Done. Gone. But Reginald, the torturer's hand rummaging inside of him, had no mourning to give.

The hand emerged from Reginald's belly. In its grip was a flat, square cardboard box, about five inches on a side. The torturer looked at Reginald, angry and almost afraid.

"*What is this?*" he repeated.

"Sorry. "I forgot that was in there," said Reginald. He snatched the box and laid it on the hard clay. Then, before the torturer could react, he shoved the bloody package into the silo filled with sunlight.

The torturer twisted the knife, his mouth curling into a snarl. Reginald groaned, but the groan was almost a laugh. Above them, in the stands, all eyes were watching Reginald. The arena came alive with muttered whispers.

"*What. Was. THAT?*" yelled the torturer. His face was enraged, the tendons taut in his neck. Droplets of spit flew from his mouth and hit Reginald in the face. The knife rose and fell, rose and fell, and the torturer's black robe became wet with spatters of blood.

Suddenly there was a bright flash from the stands as Logan's robe exploded into fire. Sparks and smoke erupted from where he'd been standing. Then the same thing happened to either side, to each of Logan's Guards. To members of the crowd. To Guards around the room, at the entrances and exits.

Beams of sunlight were lancing out of the silo and cutting through the darkness like swords. It was as if the shaft of sunlight had grown arms.

Two beams of sunlight hit the Guards holding Reginald. They spun away in pain, their faces already blistering. Maurice had told Reginald that his tolerance for sunlight would decline with age, and that the episode in the car his first week would have very seriously and very quickly incapacitated an older vampire. And apparently it was true, judging by the chaos he saw around him.

Reginald, with his younger eyes, forced himself to squint into the light of the silo so that he could watch Nikki work, tilting the shaving mirrors in her hands at anyone that tried to intervene or flee.

"Get this one!" Reginald yelled, gesturing with his head.

Nikki aimed one of the reflected beams at the torturer. A great glut of sparks erupted from his face and neck, and then he screamed and rolled away, clawing at his boiling skin.

Reginald pulled the machete out of his chest. Then, despite the silver chains, he found he was able to summon enough strength for something a human could do, and brought the blade down on the torturer's neck. The blade went through him as if he were made of paper and twigs, and then he exploded into fire that smelled like brimstone. Knowing time was not on their side, Reginald didn't pause to gloat. He cleaved the necks of the still-sparking Guards who had been holding him down, then seized a set of keys from the ash and began to free himself. In the stands, he could see Maurice doing the same.

Nikki trained the beams on Logan. Smoking and burning, Logan staggered backward and fell heavily into his throne. There was a blur as Maurice appeared behind him. With the flat of one hand, Maurice struck the back of the throne. It exploded forward into a million tiny wooden stakes, into Logan's body.

Then there was a ball of fire, and the Deacon was gone.

"I claim Deaconship of this Council," Maurice's voice boomed. He looked down at Reginald and, as best he could through the glare, at Nikki. "And, I pardon the prisoners."

He reached behind the remains of the throne and pressed a button, and the darkness returned.

# RUN

OF COURSE, IT WASN'T GOING to be quite that easy.

Logan had led the Council for nearly five hundred years, and while tradition did say that ascension happened through assassination of the Deacon, a lot had changed since that tradition had last been tested. The Guards were used to protecting Logan, and Maurice had said from the very beginning that the Council wouldn't suddenly accept Maurice's authority — assuming the three of them managed to pull off this little caper in the first place.

By declaring himself in front of the cameras, Maurice had recorded his intention in the official record. It was likely that after things settled down, after the events of the day were analyzed, he would be determined as the rightful Deacon — but for now, he was just a murderer.

So they ran: the two thousand year-old Deacon claimant, the human woman, and the mastermind.

"We got lucky," said Nikki, comfortable at an easy jog.

"No," said Reginald, who was already huffing and puffing. "None of it was luck."

Reginald had studied every page of every publicly available Council transcript and had watched as much video as he could find time for. The Vampire Council, which went to such great pains to be unpredictable in its location, was utterly predictable in its proceedings. The layout of the arena and the sun chamber was always the same. A wanton creation charge laid on top of a death sentence always resulted in torture, and the torture ritual never changed. The Council always had spies who were shockingly thorough. Surprise witnesses were always called, revealing some secret the convicted party didn't realize the council had known all along. It was boring, like clockwork.

Nothing that had happened today had surprised Reginald. It had all gone exactly as it always had... until the fat vampire did something that no thin vampire ever could, by hiding a weapon inside of his body.

They ran down the long underground corridor that connected the Council's current location to an abandoned parking garage. Guards came in waves. Maurice was able to hold them off, but that would change when they began attacking in greater numbers. Reginald had predicted that would come next. Because the fugitives couldn't escape into the sunlight, the Guards could drive them into a corner, where they'd be able to concentrate their remaining numbers into one large assault. Maurice was powerful, but Reginald had always been useless and they'd have realized by now that Nikki was human. Maurice couldn't take on more than five or six at most.

Behind Reginald and Nikki, there was an explosion as Maurice decapitated another Guard with his hands.

They reached the garage staircase and began climbing. It was slow-going, but the Guards were still only coming in ones and twos. A few minutes later, they exited the stairwell at the fifth floor, and walked into the southeast corner, where Reginald's cousin Walt had left a car with an ignition key stowed under the floor mat.

It was impossible for anyone to decipher a 128-bit encryption key and hack the Council algorithm. But the world had never seen a mind like that of Reginald Baskin.

When they reached the car, Maurice and Reginald climbed into the trunk. There was a roll of duct tape inside in case the trunk turned out to have any light leaks. The trunk itself was cavernous. Walt was only slightly smaller than Reginald, so Reginald had told him to rent a car with a trunk big enough for two Walts, just to be sure.

Nikki pulled the car out of the parking garage and stopped when they were safely out into the blinding midday sun. Then she reached back and pulled up a small knob to fold down the right side of the rear seatback, giving access to the two vampires in the trunk.

"Damn, Nikki," said Maurice. "That's bright up there."

"And hot," said Reginald, who was already sweating.

"Screw you guys," she said. "I just risked slaughter by about a thousand vampires on an errand that didn't originally involve me. I'm for damn sure going to have someone to talk to on the drive back."

"You did great, Nikki," said Reginald. "Thank you. And Claire thanks you. Or will, when we pick her up."

"I just can't believe nobody could... I don't know... *smell* me."

"You carry human blood for a few days after you're first turned," said Maurice. "They'd expect you to smell like a human."

But really, it was simpler than that. A lot of Reginald's plan relied on logic, but a lot of it also relied on human nature — or, in this case, vampire nature. People were arrogant, unable to see things from a point of view other than their own, and hence always saw what they expected to see. That's why the Guards who came for Nikki hadn't sensed her humanity.

*Of course* Reginald would turn Nikki so that she could protect the little girl in his and Maurice's absence. *Of course* Reginald would never think that the council knew about Nikki. The Council thought it had "caught" Reginald and that it had "caught" Nikki. The predator always underestimates its prey. Having been prey for all of his life, it was a lesson Reginald knew well.

"You did great," Reginald repeated. "Great acting. I thought you were really scared up there."

"I *was* scared," she said. "Scared that they'd do something you hadn't predicted. Scared they'd discover that my fangs were fake and filled with those dumb ninja powders. Scared they'd chase me when they caught me, and wonder why I couldn't run faster if I was supposedly a vampire. Scared they'd outright kill you before you could get those mirrors out of your stomach. Scared you wouldn't grab them from the guy in time, or that you wouldn't push them close enough for me to reach. Scared I'd hit Maurice with one of my sunbeams. Scared you'd gotten the location wrong and that we'd turn out to be somewhere else, with no car, surrounded by angry vampires whose leader we'd just assassinated."

"Then you did brilliantly under pressure," said Reginald. "And you saved at least two lives today: mine and Claire's.

"And probably mine," said Maurice. "I had a treason trial coming up with at least three counts to it. But now look at me; I'm the *pres-o-dent*." He imitated Yakov Smirnoff. "What a country!"

Nikki had a map beside her but didn't seem to want to look at it while driving. "How much farther before I turn?" she said.

"To Claire?"

"To the tanning salon. Yes."

"Left at 451, one mile, right on Hollister. It's 14501." Reginald had memorized not just the route but the entire county map.

They were headed to a tanning salon at which Walt had left Claire. Reginald had found it nearby via an internet search and had chosen it because it had received five citations from the state for overpowered tanning booths and for leaving tan lamps in plain sight to provide what the staff called "an ambient tanning experience." It was a busy enough place that Claire could read a book in the lobby all day long and pretend to be waiting for her mother, all the while basking in illegally high levels of ultraviolet light. The UV levels were high enough that Nikki would have needed to be the one to go in and get Claire even if it were nighttime, because Maurice and Reginald would have come out Kentucky fried.

After they'd retrieved Claire and told her a scaled-back version of their trial-and-escape story, she said that maybe she wasn't ready to become a vampire yet after all. She was, however, very happy to see Nikki and Reginald and to meet Maurice, who she confessed she'd heard a lot about.

Two hours later, they were all at a temporary safehouse — a weekly motel room which, through a computer error of some sort, had been paid for by an American Express card belonging to one Todd Walker.

And the waiting began.

# BLOOD

TWO WEEKS OF HIDING, ONE reluctantly-conferred Deaconship, and two dozen pounds of raw ground beef later, they left the motel as free men and women. Reginald found himself still hungry, and growing increasingly intolerant of dead blood.

Maurice went out and hunted during their hotel stay, but due to Reginald's terrible hunting record, Nikki offered Reginald her neck for feeding. The idea was simultaneously intoxicating and improper. They'd shared room and bread and board for two weeks, and they'd played endless games of euchre after teaching Claire the game, but there seemed to be something simmering between the two of them that had begun on the night Nikki had watched Reginald play the piano. Reginald didn't want to jinx it. And besides, it felt like pity. If the possibility of a free, mutually satisfying exchange of blood was possible down the road, he wanted to wait for it, impossible though it might seem.

So he waited. He kept eating raw meat, his throat increasingly burning for the real thing.

Maurice, Reginald, and Nikki returned to work on the following Monday. Berger gave them all an earful, accusing them of conspiracy and abandonment and disloyalty. The company had been forced to scramble, to improvise, and to hire expensive, premium tech freelancers. Berger's admonitions meant nothing to Reginald. He didn't care if he ended up fired. He told Berger, with zero emotion in his voice, that he'd had a death in the family. After a lot of moaning and blame-laying, Berger relented. After a lot of feather-rustling and chest-beating, he did the same for Maurice and Nikki, and over that first week back, night shift life returned to more or less normal.

The first night, Reginald went to get his 11:00 cup of coffee and when he returned to his cubicle and sat down, he was greeted with the predictable low, purring sound of a Whoopee Cushion. But this time, instead of putting his face in his hands and quietly throwing the thing away, he stood up.

Walker's perfect chin and tombstone teeth popped up over the cubicle wall. He jumped a little when he saw that Reginald was already standing, and that they were face-to-face.

"Welcome back to the nightshift, Reggie!" he said brightly.

Reginald looked deep into Walker's eyes, then grabbed his brainstem with a low, seductive voice.

"Hey, Todd," he said. "Want to come with me to the kitchen for a bite?"

## To Be Continued...

Reginald's story continues in *Fat Vampire 2: Tastes Like Chicken*. Look for it on Amazon.com or wherever you bought this book!

# Get Cool Stuff!

If you liked *Fat Vampire*, you'll LOVE the other titles being put out by Realm & Sands. Go to RealmAndSands.com to check out all of our most popular titles.

**To be the first to know about all Realm & Sands releases (and to get our exclusive, free, email-only serials!), go to realmandsands.com.**

# More By Johnny B. Truant

## For a full list of Johnny's books, visit:
### johnnybtruant.com/books

*Fat Vampire (books 1-6)*
*Unicorn Western (books 1-9)*
*Unicorn Genesis*
*The Beam*
*Namaste*
*Chupacabra Outlaw*
*The Bialy Pimps*
*Robot Proletariat*
*Space Shuttle*
*Greens*
*Everyone Gets Divorced*

# About Johnny B. Truant

**Johnny B. Truant** is an author, blogger, and podcaster who, like the Ramones, was long denied induction into the Rock and Roll Hall of Fame despite having a large cult following. He makes his online home at JohnnyBTruant.com and is the author of the *Fat Vampire* series and *The Bialy Pimps*, as well as co-authoring the political sci-fi thriller *The Beam* and the *Unicorn Western* series with Sean Platt... plus zillions of other things that we can't keep up with here.

Johnny, Sean Platt, and David Wright host two podcasts -- the Self Publishing Podcast and Better Off Undead -- both of which are available in the usual podcast places.

Johnny is also the kind of person who writes his bio in the third person.

You can connect with Johnny/me on Twitter as @JohnnyBTruant and you should totally send Johnny/me an email at johnny@johnnybtruant.com if the mood strikes you.

Also, if you liked the book you just read, I would REALLY, REALLY, REALLY appreciate if you'd leave me a review. Reviews make all the difference for independent authors.

Thanks for supporting my work!

Made in the USA
Middletown, DE
07 August 2018